*To my mother and father
and to my brother David*

One writes of scars healed, a loose parallel to the pathology of the skin, but there is no such thing in the life of an individual. There are open wounds, shrunk sometimes to the size of a pin-prick but wounds still. The marks of suffering are more comparable to the loss of a finger, or the sight of an eye. We may not miss them, either, for one minute in a year, but if we should there is nothing to be done about it.

—F. Scott Fitzgerald, *Tender Is the Night*

Once that bell rings you're on your own. It's just you and the other guy.

—Joe Louis

Both Members

of the Club

I'm standing at 33rd and Seventh where I always wait for Sam. It's a frenzy outside the Garden, people crossing the avenue, commuters running for the Long Island Railroad home, taxis picking up tourists with bags from the Amtrak trains, the windows across the street multiplying everything and, where the reflection stops, framing the scene like a movie. I'm in work boots, dark pants, a white T so I look like a black-and-white still surrounded by colors, the reds and blues and cabs moving yellow. The fights have already started.

People come out of the subway but not Sam. I watch the street. I watch the digital clock in front of Penn Station running off hours and minutes and seconds and tenths of seconds. I focus on the tenths of seconds and it's too fast and I can't distinguish the numbers and then another second's gone. The thing is to slow it down. That will be the trick for Billy tonight. To slow it down minute by minute of each three-minute round and find the openings and work them and protect his eyes. Slow it down so he can see the jabs of Antwan Davis coming.

I move closer to the exit and she's here, walking up the stairs, her body straight and lean, her eyes straight ahead. She doesn't see me. She gets to the top step and I half say, half whisper Sam. She turns and stands there.

"I want a drink," she says.

Up on the digital clock it's 8:04 and 24, 25, 26, 27 seconds.

"We have time for one."

"This is the last time," she says and starts walking too slowly. "This is my last fight. After tonight I won't do this again."

We go into Stout, busy and Friday night loud, the promise of the whole weekend, Manhattan, numbers, speed, lighting people's eyes. Sam orders a scotch on the rocks and I get a glass of water.

"It doesn't really matter if we're there or not," she says. "He never looks to see if we're there."

"He never looks at anybody."

"Then it doesn't matter."

"It matters. Let's go."

Sam finishes her drink.

"I want another one."

"We should go."

"What for? So we won't miss any of the action? So we won't miss any of the blood gushing from his eye?"

I don't say anything.

"I want another drink," Sam says. "I don't feel like going in there with a clear head."

"It's late."

"It's not that late."

She's looking straight ahead at the bottles lined neatly behind the bar and inside the Garden they're still fighting preliminaries, young pros punching and punching, some like they're on the street not in the ring, and I order another scotch. She holds the rocks glass with both hands, drinks quickly.

"You love this, don't you?" she says.

"You're done. Let's go."

We leave the bar. Two men stand just outside the door smoking and they look over Sam and the grins start in their eyes, in their lecherous mouths and one of the men says he'd fuck her.

I stop. I slow it down. Sam grabs my hand and tries to move me forward.

"Forget him," she says.

"He's just a loser," she says.

"You're doing this for you," she says.

I look at him and look at him and he moves his eyes. I give in to Sam's pull. I breathe into just walking. At the boxers' entrance a young fighter, eye purple-black, leans against the wall. I wonder if he fought tonight and if he won or lost or if he just got hit while sparring. The ambulance, like a reminder, idles ten feet from the door.

We show our passes and the guard lets us in. I pick two programs off the table and offer one to Sam, but she doesn't want it. The arena's not even half full and it's the small arena, the Theater at Madison Square Garden, not the big Garden. In the ring, the fighters circle each other throwing jabs to gauge distance. They look like welterweights. The bell rings and the fighters walk back to their corners and sit and the repairs begin, Vaseline smoothed over reddened skin, sponges dipped in water placed on each fighter's head and neck and back.

"My head's too clear," Sam says. "I should have had another drink."

Our seats are three rows from ringside. I check the program. The fighters are 140-pounders, both with two fights, both undefeated. The bell rings and the fighters leave their stools and move to the middle of the ring, then stop and circle. The kid in the black trunks, the better looking fighter, jabs, jabs, lands a three-punch combination fast, the last punch snapping the other fighter's head and sending him against the ropes. The hurt fighter tries to cover, but he's inexperienced and doesn't know how. His elbows are wide, his body open. The better fighter digs two hooks above the belt that echo dull and thick. The hurt fighter tries to grab and hold, but the fighter in black pushes him off and keeps punching. He misses three shots, then lands two to the body and a straight right that snaps his opponent's head, spraying sweat magnified by the overhead lights. The referee moves in, takes a quick look, stops the fight and both bodies relax.

It's a memory almost not mine anymore, but it comes in, a sliver of glass pushing in, so small it's more annoyance, less hurt. He's on his knees in front of me, me in his mouth, his hand on himself, the sounds coming harder, air against my cock, spit, his mouth moving, his hand moving, his breath faster and then all of it slows, stops, folded twenties in my front pocket, making money, my money, fifteen years old.

The crowd yells. They think the ref's stopped the fight too soon, but the winner ignores the boos and raises his arms. The loser's talking angry, making the mask of outrage, eyes wide, mouth exaggerated circle, but his eyes show no real desire. He finally walks to the winner's corner and congratulates the winner and the crowd claps. The announcer, taking too much pleasure in his voice, gives the official time of the technical knockout.

"He would have won anyway," Sam says. "He was stronger and faster."

"He worked the body."

"The other one doesn't look like a boxer. His face isn't hard."

Sam says she's thirsty, asks if I want something. I tell her No. I watch her walk.

The seats are filling. Three round-card girls parade by in stilettos, ring robes covering strip-club bodies they'll soon expose. Men whistle, shout. The girls wave, then sit in reserved seats to wait for the eight and ten-round fights to begin. Two heavyweights enter the ring, one a Brooklyn favorite trying to build a record, the other an overweight import from North Dakota. The bell rings. The fight's a joke. The crowd mocks the two big men, yelling at them to get real jobs. The heavyweights miss more than hit, throwing wide haymakers with no direction, and soon they're holding onto each other, mouths open, mouthpieces hanging loosely against exhausted tongues. Sam returns with a Coke. Round two starts. The local favorite knocks his man down with a looping left. The heavyweight from North Dakota shakes his head but stays on the ground until the ref counts him out.

Sam studies the ring like deciding which angle to photograph. She sits very still. She has glass slivers too, things done and done to her, maybe more hurting.

The heavyweights leave. Men stand, stretch like they

just fought. The announcer introduces fighters not fighting but here, the retired champions who've grown thick and full bellied, the current contenders resting their muscles on a Friday night. The fighters step through ropes held wide, stand on the canvas looking out of place, some in jeans, some in three-piece suits, their movements not quite comfortable. They don't know what to do with their ungloved hands. The biggest applause is for Vito Antuofermo, ex-middleweight champion. His eyes slit when he smiles. His nose is flat and layers of scar tissue cut his brows. He'd been a bleeder. His forearms are still massive, still the bull.

The ring clears. The referee tests the ropes. The bass beat of a rap song, too loud, reverberates. Sam tells me this is the last time and like a cue the movement to the ring begins.

He wears a white robe with his name printed light blue across the back and the hood of his robe covers his head like a monk going to some ritual. Covered, arms outstretched, head bent, the width of his back visible under his robe, Billy Carlyle enters.

Sam isn't looking at the ring where two new men fight. She used to photograph Billy, other fighters, the crowd, spectators straining their throats and clenching their hands into fists. She hasn't brought her camera for a while. I'm standing next to her, watching the punches, something to do until he comes from the dressing room. When the round ends I look at where we sat. The girl finishes her walk, swings the round card with a final flourish, then takes the announcer's outstretched hand, a lecherous balance for stiletto heels and three steep steps. The bell rings, stools get pulled, the fighters move, punches connect, sweat sprays, noise swells urging more.

Billy walks to us. He carries his gym bag heavy with equipment. There are eight stitches over his eye and two butterfly bandages and his cheeks and forehead are bruised raw like someone pushed his head against pavement and dragged.

"He got me tonight."

Billy's nice not to make us say something first.

I touch his shoulder. "Good fight."

"Good fight," Sam says.

Billy smiles for Sam and she turns from him and looks toward the ring.

"I couldn't get my punches off. I felt tight in there the first few rounds. I've got to start quicker next time."

A man comes over to Billy. I've seen him at the fights before.

"Hang in there, Carlyle. Get that eye fixed up and you'll be champ one day."

"Right on time," Billy says. Sometimes the south comes out in his voice.

Sam waits until the man walks away and she's alone with Billy and no one can hear.

"I want to get out of here now," she says.

"All right," Billy says. "Let's get something to eat. I'm starving."

Billy takes sunglasses from his bag and puts them on to cover his purple-rimmed eyes.

"I almost forgot these," he says.

He smiles for Sam, but she doesn't smile.

The bell rings and the fighters walk back to their corners and I see Antwan Davis standing near the exit, red track suit and tinted sunglasses, bruise-less, still undefeated, his entourage around him and a beautiful woman standing close. Billy walks on, then Sam, then me and we're outside the Garden and the smoke from a kabob stand takes over.

We walk down Eighth Avenue to the diner a few blocks away. Sam and I order Cokes and Billy gets a dish of vanilla ice cream.

"How is your eye?" Sam finally says because she needs to know.

It's too close, the loss too fresh, but I don't interfere with the two of them.

"My eye's okay," Billy says.

"What did the doctor say?"

"He didn't say anything."

"Didn't he look at it?"

"When he stopped the fight. That's when he looked at it."

"Good, Billy," Sam says.

"He looked at it. Before they stitched me up."

"What did he say?"

"Nothing."

At the end of the counter a display case rotates with

oversize cream pies and fake-looking layer cakes. A waiter cuts off a giant slice of lemon meringue that fills the plate.

"I hurt him, didn't I, Gabriel?"

"I didn't think he'd get up."

"My fucking eye beat me."

I stir the ice in my Coke. Sam takes a long straw-sip and looks up.

"You lost," she says.

"I know I lost," Billy says.

"It was a fair fight and he beat you."

"I never said it wasn't fair. I just said my eye fucked me up."

Sam puts her hands around the glass like she's trying to feel the cold.

"They shouldn't have stopped it," he says. "The doctor asked if I could see, but he wasn't even listening to me. I still could see fine."

"You'll go blind," she says.

"I'm not going blind. Don't worry about it."

"You're the one who should be worrying. They're your eyes."

I watch her take the punches the way Billy took them, six rounds behind her eyes, feeling the hurt Billy felt and feels, touching without her hand his throbbing cut, his pulling stitches. She can't keep quiet.

"When are you going to realize it's time to get out? When are you going to realize you can't keep fighting?"

"Don't give me this shit again, Sam. I'll know when."

"Look at yourself."

"I know what I look like."

"You look like hell. The last four fights you've bled. You fought a couple of nobodies before tonight and they still cut you up. We were there, Billy."

"I didn't force you to come."

"Pretty soon you'll be a body they use to build other fighters' records. They'll pay you to bleed and lose and the fans will love watching you because every time you fight your eyes will open up and start gushing and they'll be getting their money's worth."

Sam's sitting all the way forward. She catches herself, sits back in the booth.

"You done?" Billy says.

They're looking at each other, eyes to eyes, a blinking game, one eye with stitches.

"You done?" he says again.

"I'm done."

"I'll think about it when I'm ready."

"Why don't you start thinking now?"

"Because I'll think about it when I'm ready. You make it sound like I'm a loser. I'm 16 and 2. I lost two fights. Two fights and both to the same fucking guy. I beat everybody else."

"You've bled your last four fights."

"I was there."

"I'm not going to watch you anymore," Sam says. "It stays with me for days and I'm not going through this again."

Billy finishes his ice cream. No one talks. We sit in the booth for a long three minutes, a round's worth. A waiter cuts off a giant slice of layer cake. Billy gets the check and puts money on the table. He stands and puts his bag over his shoulder.

"I'll see you guys later."

"Have a seat," I say. "Don't walk out of here like this."

Billy turns around. The bruises on his forehead are more purple than red.

"Now you're giving me advice?"

"I'm not giving you advice. I'm asking you to sit down."

"No thanks. I don't want to listen to her shit anymore."

"She's just upset."

"I'm upset too. My fucking eye fucked me up."

Sam's not looking at him. Billy says Fuck it and leaves, pushes the door open too hard, door hitting wall hard, everyone looking. I feel it in my own arms, not like Sam who took the punches, but like Billy who couldn't get his punches off. The manager's talking to a waiter up front, the manager leaning over his cash register like someone's going to reach in and take his money and he's shaking his head and I know he's talking about Billy and I'm out of the booth.

"What's the problem?"

"What do you want?" the manager says.

"He put money on the table. He paid your bill. So what's the problem?"

"Why don't you join your friend?"

The manager has a red vest on, red like his robe, red like his trunks, Antwan Davis in sparkling red, red like Billy's blood.

"He was your customer."

"And?" the manager says.

"And customer's king. Don't stand there shaking your fucking head."

"It's my restaurant," the manager says.

His arms on the cash register are too low. Billy taught me to keep my hands up. We'd shadowbox in our Smythe House room, circling in the space between our beds, and he'd remind me every time I dropped my hands, every time I left myself open, to keep my hands up, protect myself at all times. The manager's not moving, not his hands, not his eyes. I punch the register. The bell goes off. The register tips and falls. The drawer bangs open. Neat rows of ones and fives and tens and twenties. The manager's backing up and Sam's in front of me telling me Let's go.

"You don't even know who that was. He's a professional fighter. You don't want to fuck with him."

"Let's go," Sam says.

The manager's backing up. The waiter's on the phone. The cops will be here in no time. I walk out the door and Sam's behind me then next to me and we're walking fast, putting distance on the diner. We cross to Seventh. The line of taxis, a yellow wedge two and three cars wide, stops up traffic outside the Garden and the horns don't stop.

"He makes you crazy too," she says. "I'm not the only one."

"Fuck that guy."

"He doesn't want people making a scene in his restaurant."

I make a fist, feel the tightness from my knuckles already swollen.

"You okay?" Sam says.

I look at her, look away.

"He's not going to learn," Sam says.

"He just fought. He just lost. It's hard to change your life just like that."

"I know it's hard."

"Do you?"

Sam doesn't say anything.

We keep walking. I'm looking for the punk from before, smoking his cigarette, talking shit, but I won't find him. Up on the clock the digital seconds fly.

"This was it," Sam says quietly. "I'm not going back there."

We're almost at the station.

"You love watching him, don't you?" she says. "Sometimes I think you wish you were in there instead of outside."

"I just watch."

"No you don't."

We stay there and her eyes don't move.

"Go on," I say.

Sam turns and walks down the stairs, her head straight, looking straight ahead. She'll be safe on the subway going uptown with all the people. Somewhere underground Billy's also taking the subway, downtown, and he'll have to sleep with hurt and loss and wake with blood on his pillow, blood which leaks through stitches and bandages, flows more easily in sleep. Somewhere else Antwan Davis is celebrating. I wonder if Antwan's head hurts or if he's pissing blood from beat-up kidneys or if his eyes are fucked up and red under tinted sunglasses or if he still feels how he felt when the fight was done and he raised his arms.

I'm standing.

They're drawing.

I force myself to go away so I won't think about now, so my muscles won't cramp like a burn, so I go to Billy and Sam and our late night walks to town, sneaking out, quiet so the house counselors won't hear, window to roof to ground then running then Billy comes in again, Billy now, his fight and his eye and it's too close.

The instructor tells me to change position.

I do.

Sometimes when I step off the platform I see what they've drawn. It's my body in all of them but not really. I have as many different bodies as artists in the room. In every class there's usually one with real talent and in those drawings my body looks most different. It's my body, but it's the artist in the lines that define my limbs, the lines more important than my limbs. Me but not me.

They draw.

I stand.

Our three reflections disappear. The subway's out of the tunnel and in front of us a band of heat makes the Brooklyn apartments look like they're moving in the middle. Everyone left in the car is dressed for the beach. Sam's taken the day off from painting. Billy's stitches are out. Sun through the window polishes the scar tissue above his eye.

The far door opens and three kids in oversized Ts and Yankees caps strut through the car. People move their feet to let them pass. The last of the three is the smallest of the three. He holds an aluminum bat, tapping the subway floor, the rhythm a methodical dare to slow their slow advance. They get to the end of the car, slide the door, move to the next car, one, two, three, bat. Billy looks past Sam at me.

"Up to no good," he says, shakes his head, mock disapproval, mock father scolding his son, then smiles.

Kids like these change in the gym. I can practically mark their progress when I visit Gleason's to watch Billy spar. New kids. Acting tough. Bad acting it's so exaggerated until they learn to use their tough in other ways, focusing violence on leather bags that don't stop swinging or opponents' bodies they hit then hug when sparring's done. Anger, hate, blind temper, that crazy switch to destroy, all of it purified into discipline and control, the best side of boxing, Billy says. But it's brutal control, which isn't what he says but it's there, when he speaks of fighting, when he describes how to hurt different parts of an opponent with precision. He can hit a man in the liver so the blood flow stops. It takes a full second before the pain registers and the man falls. I've seen Billy hook men's livers and punch at their hearts. I've seen him break a man's nose in the ring, shatter an eardrum, close an eye. I've seen him hit a man so hard, fist to jaw, the man seemed to fall asleep before he fell, his body so relaxed his face looked calm even when his head slammed against canvas. One time, me and Billy on the subway, four high school kids slow-walking the car stopped in front of us. The biggest kid, arms thick like a man's, told us to move our feet. Billy looked up at the kid and quietly, politely, calm as a movie star hard guy but not acting, suggested the kid take his friends and get off at the next stop. The kid looked at Billy and then his eyes were somewhere else, off to the side a little, and I could see he wasn't seeing anything. Billy smiled at the fear. The kid moved and his friends followed and when the subway stopped, the kids left fast. Billy turned to me, shook his head with exaggerated disappointment, said they were up to no good.

We get off at Brighton Beach. Down the steps, out the turnstiles and the sun, high overhead, makes the sidewalk sparkle. In a Russian store we buy cold water and potato salad to go with the sandwiches Billy made. We walk to the boardwalk and take off our shoes and the city beach looks almost clean.

"Where to?" Billy says.

"There's a clear spot there." Sam points to the right.

We walk across the sand and Billy drops his bag to mark the spot officially. We place towels facing the sun. Billy and I take off our shirts and pants and we both have running shorts underneath for swimsuits. Sam takes off her shorts and shirt. There's nothing self-conscious about the way she moves, folding her clothes and putting them in her bag, taking out a bottle of suntan lotion, squeezing the lotion onto her palm and rubbing it into her arms and shoulders, and if she took off her swimsuit, the white top, the striped bottom, she'd be just as comfortable. From every angle, Sam is beautiful.

"He should put some lotion over his eye," she says.

Billy's already down by the water, walking in, thigh deep.

"You'd think he'd know that," she says. "You'd think he'd know you're supposed to keep fresh scars out of the sun."

"You missed your calling. You should have been a cut man."

"It's not funny."

"Let's have a good day today."

"I want to have a good day."

"Then we will."

Billy comes back and tells us the water's freezing. He puts his cold hands on Sam's ankles and she says Stop, kicking, trying to pull her legs away, trying to have a good day, and Billy laughs his kid laugh.

I lie back and close my eyes. I listen to the sounds of people talking around me, of music muted by earphones, of kids playing, of waves.

I wake and sit up and their two towels are empty. They're past the waves, treading water and talking and Billy laughs and I'm glad she's keeping it light. They swim back to shore. I lie back and wait for Billy to block the sun. The light changes and cold water drips on my chest, a quick shiver in the heat.

"Wake up," he says.

"I'm up." I open my eyes.

"You should go in. The undertow's not that deadly and the water's not that freezing. It feels great as soon as the numbness goes away. You guys want to eat?"

"I'm hungry," Sam says.

"What about you, Sleeping Beauty?"

"Sleeping Beauty can eat," I say.

Billy unzips his bag, takes out three sandwiches wrapped in foil, sticks a plastic fork in the container of potato salad and gives us each a bottled water and napkins. Billy always packs the picnic, always stuffs his sandwiches like he's afraid we'll go hungry, a residual so obvious we used to joke about it. Turkey piled with lettuce, tomato, roasted peppers, mustard, oil and vinegar, warm from the sun.

We eat and the food, sun, ocean, all smell like summer. I collect the foil and napkins. Bees circle the orange garbage can, the best they can do without flowers.

Sam peels three oranges and tells Billy he's going to burn if he doesn't use some lotion, not saying the word eye. He takes the bottle and covers himself and puts on a Ringside cap. A vendor walks by selling ice cream, long i, long e, practically singing. Billy buys three vanilla cups with chocolate swirls. The wood spoon is flat and has the flat wood taste of a tongue depressor. Billy scrapes the last syrup from his cup, a treat between fights.

"I'm going in," I say.

"Watch out for sharks," Billy says.

I walk to where the waves are breaking and swim past the swell and soon the cold feels good. I swim back toward shore and tread water. Two kids play catch with a pink ball. An old woman in bathing cap and goggles does a slow breaststroke, breathing evenly. Billy and Sam walk to the beach and dive in and swim over and the three of us tread water.

"I'm glad you took the day off," Billy says to Sam.

"I needed a day. I need many days, but tomorrow it's back to work. They're the biggest canvasses I've ever worked on. Twelve giant canvases."

"When's the show?"

"In less than three months. All of a sudden it's in less than three months."

"Pressure's on."

Billy dives under water and comes up. The pink ball skips past the kids. Billy gets the ball and tosses it back.

"Next summer I'm taking a real vacation," Sam says. "A long vacation. I'm taking a break from everything."

"Where?" I say.

"I don't know."

"Where?" Billy says.

"Anywhere. Another state. Another country. Somewhere away."

"I don't think you'll leave New York for long," I say.

"Why not?"

"You'd get restless."

"Would you?" she says.

"I don't know."

"I would," Billy says. "After living here, everywhere else is just everywhere else. I could see leaving the Big Apple for a little while, but not for much more than a little while."

"Thank you for that," Sam says. "Both of you. I've forgotten all about my trip."

"Welcome back," Billy says.

The ball skips past the kids again. Billy catches it, pretends to throw it way out into the ocean. The kids laugh and he tosses the ball back to them. Sam's looking at her hands.

"There's always paint on me. Under my nails or in the lines of my palms. It never comes off completely, even in the ocean."

"Rub it off," Billy says.

"When I take my mini-vacation I won't paint at all. I'll come back with clean hands."

"Clean hands for what?" I say.

"You're right. I'll get paint on them as soon as I get back. I actually like it. It reminds me to keep pushing for what I want."

"Maybe I should get some of that paint. What's the best color?"

"Waterproof," Billy says.

Sam holds up her hands for us to see. There's a streak of blue across her left palm.

"So much for clean," I say. "You can keep pushing and pushing and pushing."

"One hundred days," Billy says. "One percent a day. That's how long it takes a cut to heal before you can fight again. That's my clean."

"A cut's not paint," Sam says. "And you've never even thought about anything new."

"I don't need to. I haven't retired."

"Good, Billy."

"It's all good. No vacations for me."

"A little perspective would do you good."

"I don't need perspective. I put on my first pair of gloves and I saw everything I needed to see. Same as you when you picked up a paint brush. I'm not telling you about perspective so don't tell me."

"Who else is going to tell you?"

Billy lifts his hands out of the water, makes them into fists. The pinky knuckle of his right hand is flattened, a boxer's break. "Right on time," he says.

Sam swims out, a perfect crawl she learned before us, and floats on her back. Her eyes look closed, but I can't tell.

"This is the life," Billy says. "When I retire I'm going to live by the ocean. Maybe I'll move to Florida and take up shuffleboard."

"I'll be sure to visit."

"You better," he says. "Think about all those older women sitting by the pool. You think when you're older, you like the way older women look?"

"I don't know. Tell me when you get there."

"I bet you do. I bet that's built in."

Billy looks past me and his eyes narrow like he's straining to see something far away. He's facing the horizon. I'm facing the beach.

"It's great Sam got her first show," he says.

"This is her break."

"Twelve paintings. Championship rounds."

The kids throw the pink ball back and forth.

"I had some trouble at the gym," he says.

"What kind of trouble?"

"Some shit with Phil. He's supposed to be my trainer, but he started talking like he's my boss. I know what I need to do. When I make it, he'll be getting paid by me, big money, not the other way around."

"What did he say?"

"What do you think?"

"Your eye."

"See that? You are a quick study."

"Fuck off. I haven't said a word."

"I can see you thinking," he says.

"You don't know what's in my head."

"I know what's in your head. Just like I know what's in her head."

"She tells you what's in her head."

"No. She tells me what's in her head about me."

Sam swims back so Billy stops talking. He dives under water and the bubbles rise, Billy letting out breath, and then he's out of the water, all the way up to his knees, smiling like summer vacation, the boxer, the professional liar, feinting a left to throw the right, delivering softer blows to set the unexpected bomb, creating traps to expose men's hearts and heads. I see the lie. Sam sees the lie. Billy has a piece of seaweed in his hand and he swims after Sam, a playful truce splashing in the Atlantic.

I float on my back and wait for them to return and we all swim back to shore.

"Let's check out Coney Island," Billy says.

"I want to stay in the sun a while longer," Sam says.

"Later I mean."

My towel's sandy. Someone puts on a radio. Someone walks by holding a cigarette, smoke cutting salt air. Vendors walk back and forth.

Billy draws tic-tac-toe lines in the sand. Sam puts an X in the middle box and Billy takes her to a draw. They play a few more times and no one wins. Billy erases the marks with his hand and draws three grids on the smoothed sand to make the game three-dimensional. Sam beats him with Xs in the corners. Billy asks for a rematch and she beats him again. He erases the marks with his hand and draws a face with a frown on it. Sam adds a body with a few quick strokes.

"You win," Billy says.

"I saw a film clip where Picasso paints a bull on a piece of glass so the camera can focus on the paint and the brush and his hand and his face as he does his strokes. It takes him a few seconds and a few lines and there's the bull, but it's not just a quick sketch. It's the outline of a bull and the essence of a bull at the same time. That's what made him great."

"Picasso wins," Billy says.

Billy draws a circle with two sharp horns. "It's a bull," Billy says.

Sam finishes the sand sketch, creates the body, the large chest moving forward to attack a matador that's not there.

"You're the champ," Billy says.

"We're just drawing."

"I could practice my whole life and I couldn't draw like you."

"You could learn to draw."

"You're born with talent," I say.

"You develop talent," Sam says.

"You're born with it first."

"I agree," she says. "You're born with what you're born with, but without work it means nothing. After a while potential becomes a dirty word."

"What about luck?"

"I won't leave things to luck," she says.

I draw two squares in the sand. Put five dots in one. Put two dots in the other. "Lucky seven," I say.

"High roller," Billy says.

I erase the dots, put a single dot in each square. "Snake eyes."

"You don't need dice for that," Sam says.

"You're right," I say. "My eyes are slits naturally."

Sam puts her finger in the sand like she's about to draw something else, but she doesn't. She says she's going back in the water to cool off and then we can go. I watch her walk to the water and dive in and come up farther out than I thought she'd be. She starts to swim. I look at Billy and he's watching her too.

Sam comes back and shows us two mussels she found, their shells stuck together. She rubs the shells with her fingers to bring out the blue. We pack our towels. A plane flies low in the sky with a banner advertising Banana Boat Sunscreen.

The boardwalk planks burn. Kids hang around a

bench, pushing, laughing, and we put on our shoes and two girls start dancing, heads, eyes posed. On the handball courts old men play against old men, bare chested and dark from summer. Pink balls slap metallically against high cement walls.

The Cyclone's in front of us. At Smythe House a traveling fair came to town every May, set up in the town common. Kids from school worked the booths. Rough-looking roadies, tired from traveling south to north, operated the rides. Sam moved from one high school boy to the next to the next, and when she was with one of them, Billy and I wandered the fairgrounds searching for girls from other towns. We took them on rides and bought them candied apples or cotton candy. When Sam was with us we stayed with her. On the Ferris wheel, crammed into one seat, Sam between us, we rocked the car back and forth as soon as we reached the top, fooling ourselves we could fall, the fun side of danger. On the way down we laughed at the drop, the getting closer, everything sharpening, people's faces, grass, green blades and trampled dirt.

Kids wave from the carousel at smiling mothers and fathers. Kids in miniature cars beep cartoon-pitched horns. Billy says we should ride the Cyclone. Sam doesn't want to and I don't, but we follow Billy to the ticket booth. The roller coaster climbs the first hill then rushes down, the riders lifting their arms and screaming like they've won something.

"Come on," Billy says.

"We did it last year," Sam says.

"So what? It's great. It gets your adrenaline working."

"You miss your fix?"

"Don't," I say. "Let's go on. It was fun last time."

We stand in line. Billy takes out a fold of cash to buy three tickets. I tell him the ride's on me.

"I made some decent money last fight," he says.

"You earned it."

"So let me pay."

"You made the sandwiches. If I'm going to hurtle to my death I want to pay for it."

"What about my death?" he says.

"I'll pay for that too. And Sam's."

Billy pockets his cash.

The roller coaster climbs to the top of the first hill, pauses, then drops. People scream, wood rails rattle.

"When was this thing built?" Billy says.

"Too long ago," Sam says. "Even up close it seems like from another time."

"Don't worry. Except for all the rusted metal, it looks sturdy enough."

"We'll find out soon enough."

"It was nice knowing both of you," I say.

I pay for tickets and we wait in line. The ride stops, everyone gets off, we get on, me in the last car, Billy and Sam in front of me. The cars make the slow climb to the top and I look over the grounds and the beach and the ocean and it's the moment before. The drop's in my crotch and throat. Billy lifts his arms. Sam's hair touches my face. We whip around the track and the drops become less and less and the ride slows and stops.

The Ferris wheel circles. The Tilt-A-Whirl spins. The monsters in front of the haunted house move in stuttered fits. Video games. Shooting games. A game called *The Boxer*. Sam leaves it alone. A kid throws a sloppy punch at a speed bag and numbers light up. A hawker yells for us to try our skills at darts. Billy buys five, aims, breaks two balloons attached to a board, not enough for a prize.

"Sorry," he tells Sam. "I wanted to win you a stuffed animal."

"I don't need a stuffed animal. I don't even want a stuffed animal."

"I'm giving it another shot."

"There's the spirit," the hawker says, darts bunched in his hand.

Billy pays, focuses, throws, breaks three balloons. The man asks which prize and Billy chooses a small bear. It's white like a polar bear, but its face isn't cold. Sam kisses Billy's cheek and puts the bear in her bag headfirst.

We walk back to Brighton Beach. Sam's face glows

with a little sunburn and Billy's shoulders and back are red. The plane with the Banana Boat ad flies the other way.

Trailers and trucks fill the street and the familiar electric cables run up and along the boardwalk, lights pointing at a restaurant front, and there's the camera. I'm so far from Hollywood and I don't want to watch. The assistant director calls Action. Two actors walk out of the restaurant and speak to each other and I don't recognize the actors and can't hear their lines and they shake hands and move in opposite directions. The assistant director calls Cut and the two actors stop walking.

"What movie is this?" Billy says.

"I don't know."

"Let's go," Sam says.

"I never saw those guys before," Billy says.

A hand on my shoulder. I turn around and a man stands there looking at me. His wide face is dark brown and there's a scab on his nose where he must have fallen and he holds a bottle in a paper bag. His eyes are glazed, more red than white, blue irises lit. I smell alcohol.

"You actor?" the Russian says.

"Not today."

"Good actor?"

"He's a great actor," Billy says.

"You in movie?" the Russian says. He's focused drunk. It's him and me and nothing else. "You movie star?"

"No. I'm not."

The Russian smiles. The Russian laughs.

"So," he says. "So you not movie star. So, so, so. So what?" He hands me his bottle.

"No thanks."

"You look movie star." He lifts his bottle in the air, then drinks.

"Sign this guy up for your agent," Billy says.

The assistant director calls places for the next take and the Russian starts yelling Good actor, good actor and a production assistant, fingering his important headset, rushes over and tells the Russian to keep his voice down. The Russian lifts his bottle and yells Good actor and the assistant tells him they're trying to finish the shot. The Russian's eyes are back on me. He drinks, wipes his knuckles across his mouth, leans in, breathing whiskey, not vodka.

"You movie star," the Russian says.

"Thank you," I say.

"Good actor," he says.

People in the crowd are staring. I don't give them anything. The Russian starts yelling and a crew member comes over and gives him a dollar to leave. The Russian pockets the bill and walks away holding his bottle high in the air.

The assistant director calls Action. The two actors come out of the restaurant, do their lines, shake hands, part.

The assistant director calls Cut.

Sam's watching me.

"Let's go," she says.

"These people don't know what they're missing," Billy says.

The actors walk back to their places for another take.

"Give the director one of your postcards," Billy says. "You got one in your bag?"

"The film's already cast."

"Badly cast."

"Let's go," Sam says. "Let's get back to the city."

I stand.
They draw.
The instructor tells me to change position.
I do.

Usually there's someone with overdeveloped muscles on the bars in Washington Square talking too much about the best exercises for lats and biceps and triceps and they're too stupid to know it's in the head, but today there's no one and I finish my dips, get off the bars, do one hundred sit-ups with my feet tucked under the dog-run fence, punching my stomach during the last twenty.

I didn't hear from him for a week. Then my phone rang and Billy said Bonjour, calling from France, excited, telling me about a fighter from Gleason's who'd gone to Paris to build his record, telling me as soon as he knocked out some French fighters he'd come back to New York for another shot. I asked about his eye and Billy told me to drop it, I sounded like Sam. I told him to come back and he said No.

I catch the cross bar and hang until my arms burn and my hands hurt from the pull. Billy called again this morning. He told me Paris was treating him right, that he'd hooked up with a promoter and had a fight date, that French women were fine even if he couldn't really talk to them, that I shouldn't worry and to tell Sam not to worry, that he didn't think these French guys could touch him in the ring.

I walk to Christopher and take the subway to 79th. La Caridad is almost empty, a window table free. I sit facing downtown and the sun's in my eyes and most people are walking downtown, more backs than faces.

I see Sam across the avenue. I watch her wait at the corner and then cross Broadway. Her posture's perfect. When she paints on big canvases, taller than she is, wider than her stride, she stretches and bends and kneels and jumps, dipping thick brushes into cans of color, then reaching high, arm muscles flexing, leg muscles taut, the points in her shoulders and her clavicle defined. She's physically exhausted when she finishes her days. Sam comes into the restaurant. If she saw me watching she doesn't let on. She sits down and puts her hand next to mine.

"You're tan," she says.

"I've been in the sun."

"I've been in the studio. I have that studio pallor going."

The waiter sets down two water glasses and two menus.

"Billy called again. He has a fight lined up."

"That was fast."

"He sounded excited."

"Billy always sounds excited. He's still a child that way."

"I guess we're all grown up then."

"I didn't say that. There's nothing wrong with getting excited. I'm showing my work in a Soho gallery and I'm excited about that."

"He's showing his work in a Paris ring."

"He's a child because he doesn't think about the repercussions of anything he does."

"You're wrong."

"I can't picture him there," she says. "Maybe I don't want to picture him there."

We look at the menus, half Cuban dishes, half Chinese. Sam orders a plate of rice and black beans and a cafe con leche and I order pork chops and a side of plantains. The waiter brings Sam her coffee. She adds one sugar. Her hands aren't as dark as mine.

"The number one export of Cuba is sugar," Sam says.

She's looking at the paper placemat, a map of Cuba with a list of facts down the side. Population. Size. Language. Exports.

"The name Cuba comes from the Indian word Cubanacan, which means center piece," she says.

"The national drink of Cuba is the Cuba Libra."

"You're making that up."

"Rum and Coke. With a twist of lime."

"I was just reading about one of their artists, Wilfredo Lam. He was a Cubist, a Cuban Cubist, but he left the country when he was twenty-one. He was before Castro's time, but even then artists didn't exactly flourish in Cuba."

"Castro boxed."

"That's a fun fact. Maybe Billy should have gone to Havana."

Sam looks out the window, more faces than backs, then back at the placemat.

"The national symbol of Cuba is the Royal Palm," she says.

"I went to the gym Saturday and spoke to Phil Brice. He didn't know Billy had gone to France."

"What did Phil Brice say?"

"He said Billy walked out on him. Phil told Billy he wouldn't train him anymore until he went to an eye doctor and Billy got angry. He cleaned out his locker and left."

"He'll go blind," she says and her eyes go another kind of blind, not letting anything outside in, years of practice taking light from her pupils.

"That should be exciting for him," she says. "He can wear tinted sunglasses all day long and when he walks down the sidewalk tapping his cane, everyone will scatter."

"I'm thinking of going to Paris."

"To do what?"

"To stop him."

Sam takes the napkin from under her knife and fork and puts it on her lap. She lifts her coffee cup with both hands. I look out the window at the cars and taxis and all the people.

"It won't make any difference if you go there," she says.

"It might not."

"I can't go with you. I have my show in a few months and I already feel like I'm behind and I can't just leave. And last time was the last time. I'm not going to watch him fight again."

"I hope that's it. I hope it's because you can't watch."

It's six hours later in France, dinner time not lunch where Billy is. The people at the next table get up. A waiter re-caps the hot sauce, slides the oil and vinegar bottles to the center of the table and clears the plates.

"What would you do about acting?" Sam says.

"Whatever."

"That's a good word."

"Whatever. I've had some bad auditions."

"Your next auditions will be good."

"The last time I was in rehearsal I didn't want to be there. I was acting and watching myself act at the same time so it was shit acting and I didn't even care. I didn't even care if I felt the high or not. All of it, all of what I thought I needed, I didn't need it."

Sam sips her coffee, both hands on the cup, deciding if she should keep talking or not. I know her that well. And I think how I've forgotten I know her that well. She holds the cup in front of her mouth.

"Make sure," she says. "I think you still need to be loved."

"Maybe it's time to get rid of that hard childhood shit?"

"It's not shit. It's there. If I paint and you act because of our pasts, I think that's fine."

"But fighting's not fine?"

"We can't get hurt like that."

"When he wins, people love him. It's the same need for love we supposedly crave. And it's not love. I don't know why you call it love. It's attention or something connected to attention. Whatever it is, when he wins it's complete."

"Are you trying to convince me or yourself?"

"I'm not trying to convince anyone. I know what I see. You've seen it too."

"I saw it when he won."

"Even when he loses, there's something complete there. It's his own."

"Billy hates to lose," she says.

"Yes, he does. So do I. Or I used to."

"You haven't lost yet."

"I'm losing. Just like Billy."

"You're not losing like Billy."

"The only one not losing is you. He lost two fights. I've lost too many auditions to count. You didn't mind watching him fight so much when he won."

"Don't accuse me of that."

"Smile, Sam."

"What?"

"Smile for me. Give me that smile. The one that says you'll do anything to win."

Sam smiles. On cue. I've seen her smile at men, men who might help her, and then, sometimes minutes later, she and the man aren't there. Wherever they were they've gone somewhere else. She's smiling, but her eyes are flat. She's letting me know it's an act by giving me half the act, her mouth, not her eyes.

"Great smile."

"It is," she says.

"You win."

She puts the smile away. Her eyes weren't in it anyway so it happens like that.

"Don't worry," she says. "It would never work with you."

"That's because I know you."

"Exactly," Sam says. "And I know you. Both of you. But it would never work with you."

"A couple of boys you went to school with starting to lose."

"He's getting hurt. You know there's a difference."

"Are you getting hurt?"

"No."

"You're that sure?"

"Whatever I'm getting, I'm not bleeding."

"I don't know. He's doing everything he can to keep fighting and win."

"But he doesn't have to smile. That's what you're insinuating."

"He relies on other things."

"He's still losing," she says.

"If we were painters you wouldn't be anywhere near us, would you? We'd bring you down. Just being around us would get in the way of your art world plans."

"Fuck you."

The waiter brings the food. Sam spoons beans over her rice. The pork chops are thick but tough. She keeps her eyes on her food, on the window, away. The waiter refills my water.

"It was easy when he first started," Sam says.

"He was undefeated."

"I'm talking about something else. There was something choreographed in the way he was always moving forward. There was something clean about it. That's why I wanted to photograph his fights. It was brutal and clean at the same time. Now there's too much blood for it to be clean anymore."

"There's blood in everything."

"I do my work. The rest will happen. The rest is happening."

"You'll make sure of that."

"Yes. I've always admitted it. I'll do whatever it takes."

Sam's eyes are her kind of blind, blind to everything around her but her, and I slit my eyes to my kind of blind, not focusing on something more like Sam, just making everything nothing, a layer of blur right in front of my eyes, folded twenties in my front pocket nothing, ending an audition nothing, walking a runway slit-eyed nothing, standing naked while they draw me not me.

"You should too," she says. "If you have the chance, take it."

"Maybe I don't want to use anyone anymore. Or owe anyone."

"Using and owing are very different. If you use the right people, the ones that want to be used or are used to being used, you don't owe anything."

"No repercussions."

"Not if you understand what it's for," she says. "When my show opens it will be my work on the walls. That's all that will matter."

Sam keeps her eyes steady to show me she has no doubts.

"And then the work is everything," she says.

"A day after the fight he's doing push-ups so he won't lose a step."

"It's not going to happen for Billy."

"He doesn't believe that."

"Then why would you go to Paris? If he's doing the right thing, why don't you leave him alone? Let him fight. What's the point of going over there?"

"You know the point."

"Tell me."

She lets some of her blindness go. I open my eyes to more than slits.

"Our past together's the point."

"I thought we're leaving the past out of things."

"Some things."

"You can't choose like that," she says. "Sometimes I think you like seeing him bleed."

"I hate seeing him bleed. But I wish I had the equivalent. If I bled that much maybe I'd know, maybe that's the sign I'd need to stop and walk away completely."

"He should take it as his sign."

"You wouldn't."

"I'm not getting hurt. Literally. Anatomically. That's the difference. He can go blind."

"Man on man. It has to be hard to walk away from that. In the ring, it's just you and the one in front of you, but really it's just you. Nothing else and nobody else."

"The one in front of Billy beat him and beat him again and if they fought a third time he'd beat him a third time. He can go to France and come back and Antwan Davis, and all the fighters in the world who are better than Antwan Davis, will beat him."

"Probably."

"So why are you fighting me?" she says.

"Maybe I'm fighting me."

"Don't. And don't fight me so much."

I put up my hands, fists in front of face. When he lifted his fists she'd swing, trying to get to him and he'd laugh, his hands would drop, she'd hit him sweet rough and I'd watch them play but we never played like that, me, Sam, and we never told him, never how we took money from men, but he told us of his men, his father, the man from his first foster home, not about their cocks but about their fists, about when he knew, just knew, his arms full of school fights and push-ups all day, and then Billy lifted his hands, not to deflect, not to take it just take it, but to hit, no more taking without giving, the opposite of us, taking for giving. It's his memory but mine too, mine from his telling, and I see it, see the men finally paying, not like money for me, not like money for Sam, but paying, his father first, the man from the foster home second, Billy giving, Billy beating, adult legs skidding against floor, trying to slide away, crawl away and Billy hitting, hitting, blood so dark, so slippery, so much of it.

"I'm not going to punch you here," she says and sits back in her chair.

I put my hands down.

Sam looks out the window. The waiter clears our plates. The sun's bright outside and everyone walking up Broadway wears sunglasses.

"Where is he staying?" Sam says.

"On top of the Eiffel Tower."

"Do you know?"

"I'd be able to find him when I got there. There can't be too many boxing gyms in Paris."

"And then what?"

"I'll see."

"How could he do this?" she says. "How dare he?"

We saw a death fight. Billy saw the end of it. He missed the early rounds, showering after his own fight, his fifth fight, five wins, no losses, five knockouts, sure he'd be middleweight champion of the world. We were ringside. Two skilled lightweights went at it hard from the opening bell, combinations thrown and landed back and forth, the crowd standing at the end of every round and every round looked even. In the eighth one of the lightweights got hit with a right that ripped his head back and sent him falling to the ropes. The ropes kept him up, but his hands were down and he got hit with clean shots to the head, too many shots before he fell. The hurt lightweight didn't want to quit and he bravely stood at the count of nine. The referee let the fight continue. But the fighter's legs were gone and he couldn't keep his hands up and the other lightweight knew how to finish a fight. He came forward and landed a hook to the body and three right hands to the hurt fighter's head and the beaten lightweight's eyes went dull and everyone at ringside saw he was out on his feet. The man fell slowly, his body crumpling by pieces. In the frenzy of victory the standing lightweight couldn't stop. He landed a final right that connected against the falling fighter's head just as his knees touched the ground. The punch seemed to separate the man's head from his neck and then he fell forward and his head bounced off the canvas and he lay still. The doctor went into the ring and a corner man took off the fighter's gloves and finally, after ten minutes, the fallen lightweight was able to stand. The crowd applauded. The doctor left. The fighter started walking across the ring to congratulate the man who'd just beaten him. But in the middle of the ring he stopped, his legs twitched, his eyes went into the back of his head and he fell. The doctor rushed in. The paramedics rushed in. The crowd was standing, trying to see. The paramedics hooked the fighter to a respirator and put him on a stretcher and carried him out of the ring, past me and Sam and Billy. The fighter's eyes were half-open and the respirator blocked most of his face.

After the fights ended we went to Roosevelt Hospital. The fighter was in a coma. Billy and I stayed in the emergency room for an hour. The fighter's mother was there and every few minutes she'd scream, just scream without words. Sam went outside the hospital when she heard the mother's first scream. We didn't follow her out. Billy looked at me. His eyes were unmarked then. He was very calm.

"It's part of the game," he said.

I knew then that Billy would be able to kill someone in the ring and keep fighting. It was part of boxing, an unspoken concern for every fighter every time the bell rang. The lightweight died that weekend. The way it usually went. A fighter went down. The brain didn't stop bleeding. The coma didn't end. The decision was made. Life support was removed. Four weeks later at the next fight card, the fallen fighter's name was announced and everyone stood while the time keeper rang the round bell ten times. Billy fought that night and knocked his man out in the first.

I remember the death fight whenever Billy steps into the ring. I see the lightweight walking across the canvas, then stopping, his legs shaking, his body falling, the dull look of his half-open eyes as they carried him out. I saw the lightweight when Billy called from France. Sam must see him now, his half-open eyes so far away, and her hands are around the coffee cup and she's looking down.

"How dare he?" she says again.

"I have to go there."

"Fighting in Paris," she says. "So romantic."

I don't say anything.

"When would you leave?"

"I have to get there before he fights."

"Stupid. He's so stupid sometimes."

I look out the window at the people walking past.

"I have some money," Sam says. "It's not really my money. He used to insist on helping me out. He said he didn't want me working while I painted. I put most of it away. This would be a good time to use it."

"I have some money."

"You could buy your plane ticket. You wouldn't be leaving New York if it weren't for him."

The waiter puts the check face down. I put money on the table. Sam's looking at me and I look at her and we stay there and then I look away.

We leave the restaurant. She says she has to go back to the studio. I don't have sunglasses and I narrow my eyes to the sun. We take the 1 train downtown, sit next to each other without touching. Behind Smythe House there was an old cemetery the three of us sometimes walked through at night. By day it was the high-school make-out spot, but the three of us went there to get away from the crowded house. One night Billy had too much homework and Sam and I left the house alone and walked to the cemetery. It was dark there and quiet and the grass had just been cut so the air smelled like the beginning of summer when night starts late. We were walking and then we stopped walking, just stopped at the same time. We stood still. She moved to me. She kissed me soft then hard. We held each other and then I moved her away. It was the three of us and this was outside the three of us like breaking a rule. We walked back to Smythe House without touching. Before we went through the side door Sam took my hand and pressed it hard and I pressed her hand back hard and that was all.

The subway slows at Christopher Street.

"He'll fight anyway," she says.

I stand and Sam looks up and the train stops.

"Tell me when," she says. "I'll see you off at the airport. And I want to give you that money."

"The number one export of Cuba is sugar," I say.

She smiles a real smile, a smile of acceptance, I think, that Billy has gone, that I need to go, not a smile of ambition.

I get off the train and still feel Sam.

It's hot inside the station. Everyone walks slowly up the stairs.

I buy a copy of *Backstage* at the newsstand, walk to Father Demo Square, sit on a bench, take out my pen and look through the paper. That's the actor routine. *Backstage* on Thursdays. Circle the listings. Go to auditions. Hope they're not cast.

I lean back and close my eyes. The sun makes the darkness turn orange and at the center of the orange red.

The shades are down, the lights off, the only noise the sound of engines. It's been a smooth ride, just a little turbulence out of New York. I lift the shade and look past my reflection at the wing, at the light on the wing, at the dark and the ocean's down there. I try to sleep some more.

When I look out again the sky's lighter and the sun rises from above the world touching long, thin clouds higher than the plane. Fast dawn becomes morning. The flight attendants start their breakfast stroll along the aisles. The couple next to me is sleeping and the attendant passes my tray over their bodies. The muffin's hard and cold. I eat the fruit cup. The pilot's voice wishes us good morning and tells us England is below and the weather in Paris is clear and mild. We hit an air pocket, the drop in my gut.

The plane starts its descent over the English Channel. I see the edge of France. The land gets closer. Beach. Hills. The attendants walk the aisle checking seatbelts are fastened, seats pushed back. The plane goes through a cloud, then a larger cloud, drops, levels, banks right. The engines change pitch and I see buildings and streets and cars. We're at the height if the plane crashed I think I'd get out alive. Runway, broad white lines, wheels hit, brakes take over and I feel the speed from slowing and I'm in Paris.

Passengers applaud like a curtain call. She said I still

need to be loved. She called to say good-bye. She wished me luck finding him.

I take my bag from the overhead compartment, wait, walk, single-file off the plane, long airport corridors and line up at customs. The uniformed man asks if I'm traveling for business or pleasure and I don't put on a bad French accent, don't tell him neither, just say Pleasure like I'm here on vacances, a word I remember, summer vacances. He stamps my passport. I buy a train ticket and the ride's above ground. From far away the Eiffel Tower is a picture from the French textbook we used in high school.

Gare du Nord. North Station. The train slows, stops. I put my bag over my shoulder and walk through the station, rush-hour crowded, and outside the day has started and I don't know where I am and it's different here, the colors, the width of the street, the sound of scooters, the exhaust smell, the shop signs, the roofs, the breeze, the clouds, the blue, the buses, the faces, the clothes, the shoes, the pavement and I stand still and no one's drawing and I'm alone, me watching me and me watching out, here, right here, alive and I see through everything.

Like a lens has been lifted. Like there's nothing between me and what's outside me. Like right now is stopped.

Now.

Then the lens falls back into place and the light changes, just that much, the difference between the moment after and the moment.

I pick up my bag. I walk the streets. I change money in a bank with exchange rates in the window. The teller slides change first, then counts bills, different sizes, bright colors like play next to dark green dollars with men.

I keep walking, tired but awake. Tour boats ride the Seine and I stop on the bridge, a breeze from boats or water, and look at the river and the city and recognize Notre Dame and wonder which of these quaint buildings houses a gym and which a boxing arena.

I cross to the Latin Quarter to find a room. The first hotel's full. On my way out, two students with giant packs on their backs come awkwardly through the door. They don't look happy with their travels. The next hotel has a sign, CHAMBRE LIBRE, free room, in the window. I open the door, a bell rings, the place smells of cooking. A woman in bathrobe and slippers gives me a key to see the room and it's good enough and for an extra euro I can use the shower. The water bargain seals the deal. I pay for three nights, bring my bag upstairs, lock the door, undress, get in bed. The mattress leans to the right.

Traffic wakes me. The horns sound different and I remember I'm here.

I check my phone. It's late afternoon Paris time. I walk the hall to the bathroom, wash my face with cold water, fill the sink and wash the shirt I wore on the plane, walk the hall to my room, dress, go down.

Restaurants, food stands, movie theaters playing old American movies, cheap trinket shops with souvenirs and racks of postcards and posters of James Dean and Marilyn Monroe and I narrow my eyes and pretend I'm pulling on a cigarette, easy movie-star move. I buy a crepe from a vendor. He pours the batter, waits, flips, spoons strawberry jam down the center. The crepe's warm and sweet. Some jam leaks and sticks between my fingers.

A single working boat moves on the Seine with crates stacked across its metal frame. Across the bridge a map's posted like a billboard against the wall of an official-looking building. Famous city sights are illustrated like cartoons, the Eiffel Tower with a French flag on top waving, the Arc de Triomphe drawn big and boxy. For pleasure. Traveling for pleasure. Tonight I want to enjoy Paris, act the tourist, check off attractions like that's why I'm here. Tomorrow I'll find the French Gleason's and watch the French fighters to see how hard they hit and look for him.

The Rue de Rivoli, bordered by large gardens with rows of flowers, isn't like any Manhattan avenue. The Champs Elysees is wide, the sidewalk wide enough for three couples to hold hands. Waiters dressed in black and white carry trays of drinks to outdoor tables. I go into a bar and point at what the man next to me is drinking and the bartender sets down a glass, pours a shot of Pernod, sets down a carafe of water.

I pour water into the glass and like a trick clear turns cloudy. It tastes like licorice.

I leave the bar and it's warm and my mouth's licorice-sweet and I cross a crazy circle of traffic to the Arc de Triomphe on its island of pavement. Under white lights the arch looks clean, but up close there's dirt in the cracks and pieces of missing rock. I turn around and sit on a bench facing the Champs Elysees, sloping down, and the city spreads so bright the sky looks lit and I stay until the lights seem to dim and separate.

I walk the city until I know I'll sleep.

The metro station's blue. The train coming in sounds like air escaping from a vacuum-packed can. At the next station a man with a guitar comes on, leans against the door and sings American folk songs, slurring words he doesn't understand. I transfer to the purple line. Odeon, the station near my hotel, is almost empty. The train leaves and the few voices echo and outside the restaurants are closed and it feels very late. There's a lit kiosk in the dark, posters and flyers stapled all around. He's looking back at me. The writing's different, but the colors, yellow background, bold red letters, bold black letters, are the same I've seen on posters advertising other boxing cards. Claude "Le Roi" Rondine vs. Billy Carlyle from New York. I look at the date and it was tonight.

I'm tired and not tired and he fought and there's a small store, bright, open, a man behind the register looking out, and I go in, ask if he speaks English, ask what's "Le Roi" and he makes a crown with his hands over his head. The King. Billy fought the fucking king.

I walk and the sign's still there. CHAMBRE LIBRE.

The floor of the hotel's hallway creaks. The smell of cigarette smoke comes through the door next to mine. My room isn't dark enough. I undress and lie down. The paint's fucked up on the ceiling. His face on the poster's a lie. It's a picture Sam took when he first started fighting. There's no scar tissue above his eye, his face smooth as potential. And I'm here in France, nothing to show for my time in New York, a few hours on stage, some walks on a runway, too many hours standing still, nothing close to Hollywood. The cracked box spring squeaks. The mattress leans too far to the right. I stand, throw the mattress against the wall, throw the mattress on the floor so it's flat.

The shower goes lukewarm to cold. I dress, go down, buy a croissant, walk to the kiosk to see where Billy fought. The metro clerk tells me how to get to Salle Wagram. The train's morning-rush crowded.

The front doors are locked so I walk around the back and find an open door, a hallway, an open office. I ask a man at his desk if he speaks English and tell him I'm looking for Billy Carlyle, an American who fought here last night. The man says he does not know Billy Carlyle. I ask if there's a boxing gym nearby and he says there is a popular gymnasium in another section of the city where many fighters train. He writes the name of the closest metro stop on lined paper. I say Merci. He says Rien. Nothing. I get back on the train.

Walking the stairs to the gym I smell men working hard. Inside the fighters stand too straight, too rigid, and the rhythms of their punches against heavy bags sound off. A black man does push-ups with his hands in wraps, his body defined like a pro's. I walk over and ask if he speaks English and he says he fought in America one time and speaks un peu, a little.

"I'm looking for Billy Carlyle."

"Billy Carlyle. He do not come here today."

"But he trains here?"

"Oui. In the mornings."

"I saw a poster that said he fought last night."

"Oui. Yes. He fight."

"Did he win?"

"He got a knock out. In the beginning he got cuts and then he got a knock out."

"His right eye?"

"Oui. I think also the left eye."

"Do you know where I can find him?"

"The Moroccan. Perhaps he know."

"Who's the Moroccan?"

"The Moroccan is shit," the French fighter says and smiles. There's a scar on his chin. "He is like your Don King. Comprends? He does the fight yesterday with Billy Carlyle."

The fighter tells me the Moroccan's address.

"From where you come?" the fighter says.

"New York."

"You are friend of Billy from New York?"

"That's me."

"Le Grand Pomme," the fighter says. "The Big Apple. Crazy New York."

I leave the gym to find the Moroccan. I check my phone, locate the street, take the long walk on Rue St. Denis. A few prostitutes stand in front of doorways waiting for morning customers.

The Moroccan's address is an old building with a laundromat on the ground floor. I walk the stairs to his office, number 31 with L. Habib, Promoteur written in black on the door's frosted window, knock, no answer, knock again, hear Entrez, rough. The Moroccan's built thick, gold chain around his neck, bald spot on top of his crew-cut head, barefoot in sandals, feet kicked up on a desk full of papers.

"What can I do for you?" he says in perfect English, spotting me as a visitor. He holds a cigarette tight between his middle finger and thumb and takes a pull.

"I'm looking for Billy Carlyle."

"Who are you?"

"His friend. Do you know where he's staying?"

"If you are his friend, you should know where he is staying."

"I don't."

"Mr. Carlyle left New York," Habib says. "Perhaps he is in some kind of trouble."

"He's not in any trouble."

"Perhaps you are the trouble."

"I'm just here to see him."

"He did not speak to me of any friends."

"There's no official stamp in my passport that says I'm here to find my friend in Paris."

The Moroccan takes a long pull at his cigarette and waits for me.

"Do you know where Billy's staying?"

The phone rings and Habib answers, Oui, rough, talks so fast I hardly recognize a word. Habib hangs up and laughs.

"Money," he says. "Always money."

He looks at me, then puts out his cigarette on the side of his desk. "I believe your friend is staying at the Hotel Cujas."

"Thank you. I appreciate it."

"Now you can do me a favor. Tell Mr. Carlyle I have a very good fight for him. Tell him I can pay better this time and if he does well, we can perhaps make him a fight with the French champion. Tell him to visit me soon."

"I heard Billy got cut last night."

"Mr. Carlyle won the fight."

"I know. But he got cut."

"A fighter must be prepared to get hurt, n'est-ce pas? After all, it is a hurting business."

"Did you ever fight, Mr. Habib?"

"Never. I am in the business part of this business."

"I see."

The phone rings and I leave the Moroccan's office.

I check my phone, find the Hotel Cujas, take the metro back to the Latin Quarter. The streets are crowded with tourists, Americans and Germans and Japanese, and it's almost like Fifth Avenue in summer or Times Square where it feels like no one's from New York. The Cujas looks better than the place I'm in, with a lobby and a real front desk and

the floor smells newly waxed. I get his room number and
take the elevator up.

I knock, stupid nervous, wait, hear heavy steps. Billy
opens the door and stands there in boxers. Four new stitches
sewn into scar tissue above his right eye. Two stitches above
his left eye. Billy grabs me around and holds me hard and
asks what the fuck I'm doing here and how the fuck did I
find him and what a fight I just missed, how he almost got
the shit beat out of him because this stuff his cut man used
got in his eyes and he couldn't see a thing and finally he ended
up knocking this big Frenchman out he was sure outweighed
him by fifteen pounds and looked like a killer and he can't
believe I'm here.

There's a girl in his room wearing his Ringside shirt.
Billy's smiling and introduces us like it's a game, Beatrice,
Gabriel, a friend from before New York. Beatrice says
Bonjour and picks her clothes off a chair and goes into
the bathroom. Billy asks what's new in the city. I tell him
nothing's new. He asks how Sam's doing. I tell him she's
doing fine. Beatrice comes out and Billy says maybe we'll
all go to a movie tonight, an American movie, no subtitles
this time, and she kisses his cheeks, left, right, says Au revoir
and leaves. Billy tells me not to worry, he didn't sleep with
her until last night. I'm not surprised. He always obeys the
boxing rule not to fuck before he fights. He never overeats,
never gains more than ten pounds between fights. He never
drinks. There's nothing excessive about anything he does
except train. And when Billy has his man hurt he picks his
shots and wastes nothing extra finishing the fight quickly.
Billy tells me to hold on a minute, we'll get some lunch. He
puts on a track suit and sunglasses to cover his eyes.

"I can't believe you're here," he says.

We go downstairs to a bistro. The waiter shakes Billy's
hand and seats us at a table with enough room to stretch
our legs. Billy orders two bowls of bouillabaisse, the dish
worth the trip right there, he says with the waiter smiling, and
healthy too, just fish and shellfish and vegetables, and he eats
lunch here almost every day. The waiter goes to the kitchen
and returns with two large bowls, full and steaming, and a

basket of bread. Billy asks if I like it. I tell him I do. He asks how I found him at the hotel. I tell him I spoke to a fighter at the gym and then to Mr. Habib. Billy says the Moroccan's a cheap bastard, but now that he's proved he can fight he'll make some real money and get a name for himself in France.

"What are you doing, Billy?"

"I'm fighting."

"I went to Gleason's and spoke to Phil Brice. He said you need to visit an eye doctor, a specialist. He said you weren't seeing right."

"Is that why you're here?"

"That's why I'm here."

"What else? You feel like practicing your French?"

We eat in silence. He finishes and wipes his bowl with a small piece of bread, keeping carbs to a minimum, making weight always with him. A clamshell scrapes the side.

"We have to talk."

"No we don't."

"Will you listen?"

"I'm here."

Me. Billy. Sitting at a table in France. It's absurd really, that we're here, that he's fighting here and I came here, that there's nothing fun about it, nothing easy the way it used to be easy, that we're not seeing the sites together, not meeting Paris women together, not drinking Pernod until we're laughing, our heads that cloudy, good cloudy, fun cloudy and I want to tell him Let's just have fun, let's just have easy, let's just say fuck it to everything, but I'm here and he's here and he knows what I'll say and I know what he'll say, but we're three thousand miles from where we were, and saying it here has to mean something more. I tell him to think about what he's doing. I tell him he doesn't belong in France. I tell him how Sam and I feel when we see him bleeding in the ring. I tell him maybe his eyes getting cut is a blessing, his body telling him to stop before he's seriously hurt. I tell him to be proud of what he's proved. I tell him to come home. The word sounds false in my mouth.

"Home?" he says, catching me.

"Back to New York."

"You done with your speech?"

"It wasn't a speech."

"Yes it was."

"I didn't rehearse this. I came here because I'm worried about you. Let's just get out of here and try to do something else, do something new."

"What do you mean *Let's*? You're the golden boy. It all comes easy to you."

"No it doesn't."

"You're doing well."

"I'm not doing well."

"You're doing what you want to do. You're acting."

"I haven't done much more than extra work."

"Then quit. That's what you're telling me to do. You ready to quit? You ready to say fuck it and put that away forever?"

He's looking at my eyes. Fighters know feints. Fighters know lies. I've never lied to Billy.

"I'm not completely ready."

"Welcome to Paris," he says. "Bienvenue. That's how they say it here."

"Would you listen to me?"

He pushes his empty bowl forward and keeps his hands on the table.

"What?" he says.

"Whatever I'm doing with my life doesn't matter right now. I'm not hurting myself the way you are. Your eyes are getting cut every time you fight."

"How come Sam isn't here? That's her talking. What did she do, send you over to rescue me? You her little lackey?"

"I came here myself. It was my idea."

"Sure it was."

"It was."

In his sunglasses a distorted vision of my face.

"You're lucky," I say. "Sometimes I wish I had such a defined way to know when to stop. It would be much easier to accept."

"That you lost?" Billy says.

"Maybe. Or maybe that it's time to do something else."

"Because you're a loser?" Billy says.

"I didn't say that."

Billy takes off his sunglasses, my face disappears and he leans forward, the stitches so close I see where the skin puckers where the thread goes in.

"Most people couldn't last one round doing what I do. If you've never fought you don't know. It's not your business or Sam's business or anybody's business. It's my eyes bleeding. It's my eyes and my blood and my life and it's my hard work and I'm the one who makes my decisions for me. Me. No one else."

"I'm just asking you to stop and think about what you're doing."

"You said your piece and I'm done listening. It's off your chest and you can go back to New York now. If you've got no faith that's your problem."

"I have faith in you."

"Not in my fighting and that's me. As soon as I get some wins here, I'll come back to New York strong. Then I'll start kicking some real ass starting with that fucker Antwan Davis."

"Antwan Davis won't fight you again, Billy. He beat you twice."

"My eyes beat me. You said yourself I almost had him out in the second fight."

"It doesn't matter. He won."

"I'll beat him next time."

"You're lying to yourself."

"Fuck off."

"You're lying."

The tension's in Billy's jaw and I hold my chair, wait for the punch, wait, but he doesn't do anything. He just sits there. His sunglasses on the table. His hands fists on the table.

The room is quiet. The talk is over and I feel like I do on nights when I can't seem to move. Making it and not making it. Both of us sucked in. I see the end of the death fight, the fighter stopping in the middle of the ring, his legs shaking, his body falling to the canvas for the final time. I see the skin freshly opened above Billy's eyes. I see his eyes, hurt eyes. He's as close to my brother as anyone will be.

Billy relaxes his fists. He puts on his sunglasses. He calls the waiter over and pays for the meal. I thank Billy for lunch. Billy doesn't even look at me.

"Habib. He wanted me to tell you he has a fight for you. He said if you win you might get a shot at the French champion."

"Right on time."

"That's the message."

"I'm surprised you told me."

"You would have found out anyway."

"Yes I would."

"Let me know what happens."

"Why?" he says, facing me now. "You want to watch?"

"I don't know."

"You want to check up on my eyes?"

I leave Billy sitting in the restaurant. I walk the streets, but they don't feel new.

The gym I've found is in the 18th arrondissement of Paris, a converted warehouse two floors above a narrow street. I've come here every day for a week. In the mornings I take the pink metro line and transfer to the purple metro line and get off at the Jules Joffrin stop. The city's rougher here. No postcard sights.

The gym's not Gleason's, not crowded, no contenders moving up, no champions, but it doesn't matter, I've visited gyms since Billy started fighting and I've watched him prepare. I used to think I'd use what I learned for my Oscar-winning role. Now I'm using it for itself. I'm hitting the heavy bag to hit the heavy bag. My arms and legs haven't recovered from the first day and the second, but the soreness is less now and there's something in the pain that reminds me how strong I'm getting and how strong I'll have to become and I tuck my head, shift to the left, punch.

Billy taught me the basics. I fought when I had to, before, but he taught me how to fight. To do the two-step dance that's the foundation of boxing. To bend my knees. To keep my weight evenly distributed. To stay balanced after I punch. To move my head. To shift to the side. To turn my fist at the end of my jab to cut a man more easily. To throw my right straight from my shoulder. To pivot into my hook. To punch a man's body if he's protecting his head. To make a man's hands fall to get to his head.

Billy would stand behind me with his arms around my sides, his hands around my wrists, and pull my fist back to my chin after I jabbed. I hear his voice telling me to keep my hands up. Hands up. Elbows in. Saying I'll have plenty of time to admire the damage I've done later.

He was a natural teacher, patient and slow and after, when my gloves were off and my hands shook from hitting, he'd tell me how strong my punches felt or how quick I looked and the way Billy said it felt good. He showed me how to fight to protect myself, but he also showed me so I'd appreciate what he did in the ring. Like Sam when she showed me her artwork. And they came to see me, sat through the worst experimental plays in run-down theaters, so far from anything I'd dreamed about when I flipped pages of movie-star books, but when the lights went down I heard them applauding, Billy whooping it up even when the house was empty. We were each other's best audience. I hook the bag and feel my left foot turn into the punch the way Billy taught me.

I throw another hook, move to the side, jab, throw a three-punch combination that rocks the bag. On Saturday mornings, Billy drove the house car to Holyoke to train in a boxing gym with a Dominican named Popi. Popi had gone pro, he'd even fought in Las Vegas a few times, but then his losses started catching his wins and he retired, opened a gym and trained some fighters. Whenever I went to Holyoke with Billy, Billy got me in the ring to feel the canvas against my feet, to feel the ropes against my back. He'd make sure I'd wrapped my hands correctly and he'd put on the mitts and I'd punch while he moved me around, corner to corner, until I was exhausted. After a while he said I could kick almost anyone's ass. He said it was a good thing to know. And he said I shouldn't fight unless there was no other way. I hit the bag and try to think of another way and then just hit.

I move closer, work the bag like a body, an opponent moving away, coming back. Sometimes I held the mitts for him and Billy threw combinations faster coming at me than they looked from ringside and he kept moving and his breathing never changed and through the mitts I felt how hard he hit. I took his punches and learned how to see punches coming, how to catch them like a baseball or roll with them to take off the sting and I hit the bag and I'm breathing too hard and I have to start running more miles to keep my wind. Billy used to say I'd be ready to play the fighter in any film, but there isn't a film, it doesn't matter now, I have to focus on fighting for fighting, on doing it for itself, on doing it for him. I'm hitting the bag, lefts and rights, jabs and hooks and straight right hands. The buzzer rings. The gym sounds slow. The slapping of a single jump rope remains, a fighter working through the one-minute rest.

The buzzer rings. I start slow, throw arm punches, my body not in them. Then the pull comes. I've been waiting and now it's here. It's the pull I've seen in Billy's eyes when he has his man hurt, the pull I felt when I first came to New York, walking the streets, making-it-soon in my walk, the pull I saw in actors during that one moment of film that's right there or looks right there and now I don't know if it's real or just a look, but now it's real, it takes over, becoming a high that goes above exhaustion and the bag's Antwan Davis and the bag's Billy and then it's just the black pillar hanging in every gym swinging right up to my face and I smash the heavy bag and hit and hit and hit.

The buzzer rings.

I stop. Breathing so hard it's all I hear. Throat raw. Body soaked. And clean. Cleaner than after anything.

I walk around the periphery of the gym to get my breath. I don't look at the other men. It's not like an audition and these aren't my opponents. The buzzer rings. I go to a speed bag, tear-shaped, red, hit it against its backboard, making the three-beat rhythm that's part of every gym. Billy said the speed bag did more than improve reflexes. It taught how to set up an opponent's head, the swivel working like a neck. He can keep the bag going forever, fast, making the bag blur, building the rhythm to a brutal crescendo. I hit the bag wrong. The swivel jumps. I hit the bag wrong again and it's too uneven, the movement, the sound, and I stop. It takes too long to be good at any of this.

I pull off the gloves stuck to my hands with sweat and unwrap my wraps. My knuckles are red, one skinned and bleeding. My hands shake from hitting. I choose a rope hanging on the wall and start to jump. The buzzer rings and I keep jumping, breathing hard, trying to keep the rope going, my feet catching, starting again, forcing myself to make it over the rope and the buzzer rings. Today I've done ten rounds of work. Tomorrow I'll try for twelve rounds and then fifteen rounds and then fifteen harder rounds so when the time comes I won't be killed.

I go to the lockers, undress, shower. I keep my head under until my neck loosens, my back loosens. I dress, stuff my wet T, shorts, socks into my bag. Gym sounds fill the room and linger above the stairs going down and I'm outside.

At the fruit stand the fruit woman looks at my still-shaking fingers. She takes the orange I've chosen and peels it with her knife, something I've seen her do for other fighters, a gift for men with trembling hands.

Purple line to pink line to Odeon and outside the cafes sound like vacation. I'm starving from the workout. I buy a gyro served on French bread with French fries and salad inside, the way they make them here, the difference in the details. The food. The streets. The buildings. I'm sure Billy saw the difference in the French-trained fighter who drew the same-old, same-old blood. I sit against a wall to eat. Dropped pieces of meat and fries are pressed into the cobblestones. Waiters outside the prix-fixe restaurants hawk business. I eat half the sandwich, full enough, put the rest in my bag for later, go where I have to go.

The Moroccan's sitting in the same position behind his desk. Legs up, cigarette tight between middle finger and thumb, yelling rapid-fire French into the phone. He motions with an open palm for me to sit. I look around the room, at framed photographs of the Moroccan standing next to fighters I don't recognize, at publicity shots of fighters I do recognize, an old picture of the famous French middleweight champion Marcel Cerdan. Taped to the wall, posters of fight nights Habib has promoted, the most recent with Billy's picture. Finally Habib gets off the phone. He writes something down. He leans farther back in his chair and asks what he can do for me.

"Get me a fight."

He taps a cigarette from his pack, lights up, inhales slow, exhales slow.

"Get you a fight. Is this a request or a demand?"

"I'm asking. I want to fight."

"You are a fighter now? I thought you were a friend."

"I want to fight on your next card. According to your posters you hold fights once a month."

"You are training?"

"Yes."

"Here? In Paris?"

"Yes."

"I see," Habib says. He takes a long pull at his cigarette and blows smoke through his nose. "It is not so easy. The next fights happen in two weeks."

"Just a four-round preliminary."

"Just. Comme ça."

"It's twelve minutes at most. I know you can stick me in somewhere."

"Twelve minutes can be interminable if the fight is poor."

"You're right."

"I know I am right."

Habib rests his cigarette on the edge of his desk. He opens a folder and looks over a page.

"I did have one cancellation," Habib says. "Still, these things are difficult to arrange so quickly. The pay would be very little."

"I'm not worried about the money."

"Perhaps three hundred euros. About two hundred dollars American."

"I'm in the big time."

"If I promote the fight, it is the big time." Habib

taps the ash and takes a pull. "What about the undercard of Mr. Carlyle's main event? That would be in six weeks. Perhaps that would be better, two Americans together in one night."

"No. It has to be before that."

"Why?"

"It just has to."

"Why must you fight here?"

"It's romantic. Paris and all that."

Habib smiles. He puts out his cigarette on the side of his desk.

"How much do you weigh?"

"Same as Billy."

"You have fought before?"

"Never."

"A first professional fight in Paris."

He makes a phone call and another and a third. I can't understand what he's saying, just the words American and New York and combattant, fighter. Habib hangs up.

"He is a young man from Marseille with a record of two wins, no losses. He agreed to fight in romantic Paris. I believe he has a woman friend here. The best reason of all, n'est-ce pas?"

I sign a contract and a medical liability release. Habib writes down where I need to get my license. He kicks his legs back onto his desk and picks up the phone.

"Don't tell him," I say.

"Pardon?"

"Don't tell Billy. It's a surprise. He's been trying to persuade me to turn pro for a while and I've always refused."

"I will see you in two weeks."

I stay where I am. Habib looks up, annoyed, playing the busy man, fights to promote, the hurting business.

"Please," he says and glances at the door. "I will not ruin your little surprise."

"Don't."

"Good afternoon."

I leave Habib's office and the shouting begins behind

his door. I wonder if he's telling someone about the stupid American who wants to keep his first fight secret, who thinks Paris is the most romantic fight city in the world.

I buy a postcard, find a post office, buy a stamp, use a pen on the counter to write to Sam. I tell her I've found Billy. I tell her he's fine. I tell her I've decided to stay in Paris a few weeks and that I've visited the Louvre and seen some sights and hope she's painting well. Then I sign off. Gabriel. My name looks strange to me. I read over the card and it's cold. I wonder how she'd watch me in the ring, if she'd want to take pictures or if she'd just look straight ahead and take the punches when I took them. I turn the card over. The Arc de Triomphe lit up at night, cars circling the arch, headlights blurred streaks, moving too fast for the camera.

I'm near the Louvre and want to see the *Winged Victory of Samothrace* again. In the lobby, tour groups cluster around guides holding colorful flags. I walk past them and through the long hall, marble columns, arched ceiling, giant paintings in ornate gold frames, then space. I sit on the steps to look across at the statue. Even without a head she's beautiful. Under her robe I see her body's power and almost feel the wind her wings would make if she flew. I think of Sam and summer nights and how she drove barefoot in the Smythe House Cutlass with the dent in the side, Billy in back, me next to her, her feet tan against the gas and it's just us, no other cars, the cops never here. She flips on the brights and the road lights up so far the white lines become one line and the road narrows all the way to the dark and she pushes to 100, pushes past 100 and it's this car, this piece of road, this speeding forward, windows down, wind pressing, speed pressing, loud pressing so strong it takes over.

I sit and look at her for a long time.

I get up and walk through some of the museum, don't stop at the *Mona Lisa*, her smile shielded by bulletproof glass and a constant crowd. The gift shop's near the exit. Postcards and posters and prints and calendars. A glossy art book stops me, a book of George Bellows paintings. I turn the pages and recognize the reprint of the sad-faced Firpo knocking Jack Dempsey out of the ring. It's the painting Sam showed us at the Whitney Museum when we first moved to New York, when New York was new, when we went out all the time. She showed us where George Bellows put himself ringside in the painting and Billy told us how Dempsey crawled back through the ropes and knocked out Firpo the next round.

I look at the full-page reproduction of *Both Members of This Club*. It's a slow-motion death fight. The two figures, one black, one white, are connected in the center of the ring. The faces of the crowd are clown-like, the faces of the boxers covered in shadows, the struggle frozen forever. When no one's looking I put the book in my bag. I haven't taken something in a long time. I feel the adrenaline rush when I leave the museum store and wait for the hand to grab me from behind, ready to run, but the hand doesn't come.

I walk back to the hotel. I'm tired, tired every afternoon from the morning workout. I open my bag, take out my gym clothes, take out the Bellows book, rip out the page and tack it to the wall with old tacks already stuck in the plaster. Isolated from the book, the two men struggle harder. I see the power I'll have to make my own and the danger, the danger I want Billy to see from a ringside seat.

The mirror's on the closet door. I try to see myself like the fighter will see me. I narrow my eyes, make them hard, put up my hands, tuck my head into my shoulder.

"Come on," I say to me.

I swing.

I swing again, again, fists at my face, my eyes, my voice Come on, Come on, pull spreading, Come on, me punching.

The pull leaves. Without gym sounds it's just me breathing hard.

I lie down on the mattress on the floor. I think about the fight. About the kid from Marseille with the 2 and 0 record. About what he looks like. If he's tall and wiry or short and built. About his skill. If he's any good. If he's a defensive fighter who knows about angles and how to move and slip punches, or if he's a brawler who keeps coming and doesn't worry about getting hit. If he's a trained fighter fighting for ranking or a street fighter fighting for proof. I'll be in his way for a different reason and he'll be in mine. I look at the two men on the wall and they're in each other's way but holding on too, dancing almost but killing each other too, holding for life because when they break, when their bodies separate, they'll each have room to deliver that final, fatal blow.

I need to rest. I try to stop thinking about the dance I'll be doing, about the fighter from Marseille, about the clown-faced crowd cheering in another language. I close my eyes and underneath I feel my pulse in my temples and the too-fast beat of my heart.

I go to the gym. I do the work. I feel stronger than I've ever felt. Like every fighter says before every fight. Best shape of my life.

Sometimes I think I see Billy running the streets or sitting in a café, but it's never him. I don't want to see him. Not until the fight. I called him once. He wanted to know what I was still doing in Paris and I told him I was seeing the sights. I asked Billy how he was and he asked if I really wanted to know and he said he was training hard and feeling strong and then he said it, best shape of his life.

For me it's true. And maybe for Billy it's true. But maybe not. False hope. Like sparring against a lesser opponent with headgear to protect your head and the finishing instinct checked.

I wash my shorts and underwear and socks and T-shirt in the sink, rinse them with cold water, twist them dry. I untangle my wraps spotted with blood, put them around the bedpost, slide them back and forth to smooth the creases, hang them over the closet door to dry. I look at the fighters on the wall still locked in each other's arms. I undress and lie down.

I sleep.

I wake.

I do fifty push-ups on the wood floor and rest and do fifty more.

I put on sweat pants, a thermal shirt, a heavy sweat shirt, making weight, and go down. Most fighters run early mornings, but I feel stronger later. I walk through the Latin Quarter's crowds to more open streets and start running hard to keep my breathing hard, to keep it hard work. People look at me. I run until my legs are heavy and I don't recognize the streets that are farther away than the streets I ran last night. I turn. The running takes over, running back, and I remember Billy running the track in summer and sometimes the hill behind Smythe House, up and down, up and down, and in winter he ran the high school corridors, his stride steady, the sound of running shoes against linoleum floor bouncing off lockers, sophomore beige, junior green, senior blue. The wrestling team also ran the hallways, but Billy ran alone. The closer to the Gloves tournament the more he ran and then, if he passed Sam or me in the corridor, he didn't look at us. He stayed staring straight ahead. I saw the focus in his eyes and the violence. I'm close to the hotel, a jump of distance between where I started thinking of Billy and now. I sprint, fast, faster, pushing myself more than I've ever pushed. Faster, faster, faster.

Habib comes into the dressing room, lights a cigarette, reads off a list of names, tells me I'm the third preliminary of the night and yells something at an old man wrapping a fighter's hands. The old man mumbles something back and Habib leaves.

The old man finishes wrapping his fighter's hands and comes over. He takes my hands and presses his hard fingers into my palms and over my knuckles. He says something in French I don't understand. He works his fingers over my fingers and says Corner, Me corner and I say Good, bon. The old man's face is pressed in and the scars around his eyes look like they've been cut by a dull blade. He points to two chairs and I sit across from him and rest my forearms on the chair back and the old man wraps my hands and puts white tape over the wraps and folds each hand into a fist. He puts his hands up and I hit his open hands. He opens my hands, then makes them into fists again, feels the wraps, says Bon.

I check my body. I throw punches to loosen my arms. I roll my neck. Stretch my back. Stretch my legs. Tap the leather protector under my shorts to make sure it's protective. I breathe deep. Breathe again. I try to control the fear.

I called Billy this morning. I told him I needed to see him. Billy said he was going to the fights. I knew it but had to make sure. The crowd will remember him. People will shake his hand, touch his shoulder, feel his strength. He'll get the kind of love Sam says we need. I told Billy I'd meet him inside the arena. I didn't tell him where. I shake out my arms and breathe deep.

I pace the room. The French National Anthem plays out there, then a cheer. Fighters stretch and pace and throw punches, some at trainers with mitts, some at air. All of us are fighting out of the blue corner. We're the out-of-towners, the unknowns, the ones with losing records. The red-corner favorites are in their dressing room across the hall. I wonder if their room is as hot as ours, if it stinks of mold, if the benches are chipped, if the light's yellow like fear.

Habib comes back in, wishes us Bon chance, lights a cigarette, leaves for his ringside seat. An official calls out two names for the first fight. A man, thin, all defined muscle, stops pacing and crosses himself. He puts his gloved hands on the old man's shoulders and they walk out of the dressing room. I hear an announcer's voice and the noise of the crowd and the bell rings. The first fight has started. At auditions I've learned to control what's inside me right before, to breathe into the nervousness and control it and use it to advantage. When I stand at the Art Students League I've learned to go away while I stand still. On the runway I make my eyes slits and the walking, stopping, posing, walking's easy. Now it's different. I'm waiting to fight. I will be fighting. I've watched hundreds of fights but now I'm going to fight and I don't know what that is.

I roll my neck, shake out my arms, try to relax, think about something else, another time, midnight, snowing, Billy, Sam, me sneaking out of the house, walking through town, tramping new snow paths, throwing snowballs, making angels on fresh-covered hills, grass underneath black against powder, running in darkness until our faces felt red. And later in our junior and senior years carrying a bottle of peppermint schnapps or blackberry brandy to greet the snow and cold, wandering until two or three in the morning, then sneaking back into the house a little drunk, taking off our wet shoes and walking slowly, silently up the stairs to our rooms while kids and counselors slept. We were tired the whole next day and sometimes we caught colds, but we didn't care. We didn't care about anything at Smythe House, not really. The counselors could tell us what to do, but they didn't tell us much. When other kids came to visit they'd say how great it was, how Smythe House was like camp. Sam hated when they said that, hated how they forgot who we were, why we lived where we lived. It didn't bother me. Smythe House was better than any place we'd been and we didn't have to move for three years, a commitment that felt free. And of course these kids forgot. They didn't know, couldn't know. We only told each other stories about our pasts, and they weren't even stories, but pieces really, of bad things done to us and bad things we'd done.

The stories between two not three, between me and Sam not Billy, we told the first week, new to Smythe House, the three of us not the three of us yet. I saw hers, Sam saw mine, that sliver of glass pushing in, memories that specific, and she spoke first and I spoke second and she said she hated the word, not Men, not Money, but Crazy. What other kids said, kids not like us, I'm so crazy, I'm so fucking crazy, to make them unique, fake unique, but their crazy was easy, invading their parents' liquor cabinets, eating restaurant meals and running. She told me of wanting money to pay for paint, for canvases, for food she wasn't getting, and to save to run away and she told me what she did. And I told her what I did. A man sucking my cock for folded twenties once a week. Or going to the university, to the basement in the Foreign Languages building, classes done, men sitting on toilet seats jerking off, sticking cocks through glory holes, sucking and fucking, and I'd stand there, let them see me, want me, until they opened their wallets, money for me.

The first fighter returns to the dressing room. His face is swollen. He's bleeding from a cut on his cheek. He sits on a folding chair with his gloves off and his wraps still on. His eyes aren't here. The old man leads the next fighter out, a big man with tattoos on his arms. The heavyweight keeps his head straight, eyes straight, so he won't see the beaten fighter's blood and eyes. Billy better be here. My head's numb, like it's thawing from too cold, my heart's too fast and what am I doing in France wearing shorts and cheap boxing shoes and a cut-out towel that covers my shoulders and chest to keep the sweat going and I'm next and I throw punches at the air. A trainer comes over, his hands in mitts. He nods his head. He lifts his mitts. I punch. He turns, gives me targets. I snap the pads. Jab. Jab. Jab. Left hook. Right. The crowd's yelling outside. Their yelling gets louder. Then it's quiet. The second fighter returns. Pale skin red and swollen face. Blood in his ear. Blood in his mouth. He's breathing too heavy.

The old man is waiting for me. He holds two gloves and I do what the others have done before me, what Billy still does. I put out my hands and the old man pushes the gloves over my wraps and laces the gloves and puts tape around the laces. Another man signs his initials across the tape. And my throat's tight like I can't breathe all the way and my stomach's trembling. And I hear my name.

I put my arms on the old man's shoulders and he leads me, leads me out the door and through the hallway and into the arena and it's like I'm watching a film. I see the arena and the crowd and the lights and the ring, brightest in there. I follow the old man past the crowd, past Habib, and up three steps and the old man parts the ropes and I step through. The canvas gives. I walk around the ring the way I've watched others walk and I hear his voice behind me and coming closer and he's yelling Gabriel, yelling What the fuck are you doing and I stop and turn and look down. Look at me, Billy. Look at me. He's yelling and this is what we have to watch and I tell him Look at me. Billy's coming up the steps and two security guards stop him, walk him down and I move around the ring, have to keep the sweat going, have to punch at air. The lights are hot and I can't see right like the first moments on stage. The crowd's yelling. The noise brings me back and I look across the ring and the ropes are opening, he's coming through, no robe, just shorts and skin, and he's inside the ring and he's the fighter from Marseille. Tight black hair. Thick dark brows. Clear eyes watching my eyes. I remember I have to control the fear, use the fear, turn the fear to desire. I shake my arms. I breathe deep. My head feels hot. Thick muscles stretch from his neck to his shoulders and his legs are thick. I move my legs one foot forward one foot back, one foot forward one foot back. My name's announced, loud, strange, accent off, and his name and the referee calls us to the middle of the ring and explains something in French and I'm watching the eyes of the fighter from Marseille and he's watching my eyes. The referee sends us to our corners. The old man rubs Vaseline over my face and some goes in my mouth and slides down and I gag. I wipe the grease from my mouth with my glove. The old man puts the mouthpiece in my mouth and I bite my teeth in so the pain is real. I turn from the blue corner and the old man. Across the ring he's waiting. We're waiting for each other. We're going to fight. I force myself to look. I force myself to breathe. I slow the time and stay there, right there, and I'm alive and the bell rings.

"Box," yells the referee.

I move forward and the fighter from Marseille moves forward. He hits me. He hits me again. I feel his gloves against my arms. I jab and get hit and hit and nothing's focused. The punches are dull feelings on my face, on my body. My arms feel numb and I'm breathing hard. I lunge, miss, hold him, smell him. He rubs his head in my face and pushes his forehead against my chin. I feel the referee's hand on my chest. He pushes us apart. The fighter moves to the side. We watch each other's eyes. He punches. I move. He follows. I punch and miss. I hear the crowd. I hear our feet moving on the canvas. He hits my stomach, my breath pushed out. I grab him, try to breathe. The bell rings. The referee's hand touches my shoulder and I turn around. The old man's waiting for me. Another man's putting a stool through the ropes and I go and sit.

The old man shows what he wants me to throw. My mouth hurts where my mouth was pressed against my mouthpiece. The old man rubs Vaseline over my face. He puts a cold sponge on my neck and back. I'm greased and wet and breathing hard and the bell rings and he's coming at me. We watch each other's eyes. His punches are harder now. I jab and my head snaps and my legs go weak. I can't see right and Billy's screaming somewhere. My head snaps and I feel ropes against my back. I grab him, hold him, fight my legs to stay standing. I try to remember what to do and my arms are hit and my shoulders. I'm looking through my hands. I see his heart beating under his chest. I punch at his heart. I feel my hands hitting him, he's hitting me, I'm breathing too hard, too fast, can't get my breath, raw throat. His head's under my chin. I move my head and lean. We hold each other and his breath's in my ear and I hear him breathing, hear me breathing and the bell rings.

I walk to the blue corner. The old man rubs my face, the enswell cold, metal. He shows me with his head how to move under the punch, then throw a left right. He repeats the move. Head under, left, right, un, deux, one, two. He squeezes water into my mouth. I let some coolness down my throat, spit the rest in the bucket the way fighters do. The bell rings.

I walk to the fighter from Marseille. His eyes are still clear. We meet in the middle of the ring. I jab and move. I jab and he punches and I move my head under the way the old man told me and throw a left and right and miss. I'm hit and move away. He pulls back his arm before he throws, for power, I've seen it, a moment of pulling back before he throws, and I move under his hook, throw my left, throw my right, feel the punch connect. His face is stopped in front of me and I punch and sweat comes off his hair. He grabs me. He puts his head on my chest, lifts his head into my chin. My mouth hurts, my tongue. I try pushing his head away and he puts his head into my chin again and I see his left hand coming. My nose burns. My eyes tear. I can't see. I taste blood, salty, rusty. I'm pushed back. The referee's between us. He warns the fighter for using his head, slapping his own forehead. The fighter from Marseille nods and the referee moves away. We come together punching. He hits my face, my neck, hooks my arm and my arm goes numb. I'm breathing hard. I'm swallowing blood. I spit on the canvas, red spattering blue. I punch and punch and he pulls back his arm and I'm not balanced and my arms aren't up and he's throwing the punch.

Like light. Like I'm drunk. Like the floor's moving

forward. Like I want to move so I won't fall back but my feet won't move.

I move my arms. I hold him. I feel his punches against my sides, ropes against my back and he's against me, pressing me into ropes, too heavy. The bell rings far away and the weight goes away and I'm alone.

I see the stool coming through. I force myself to walk, just walk, walk to the corner, turn around, sit. The old man's in front of me. He's rubbing the place I got hit. He's stuffing shit up my nose. Someone's pressing cold against my neck. The old man's telling me something but I don't know what the fuck he's saying and I'm telling him to stop stuffing shit up my nose and he's not listening. I hear screaming behind me. It's Billy. He's telling me to throw the right hand, he's open for the right hand, I can kill him with a right hand and I push the old man's fingers from my face and swallow blood chunks sliding down my throat and turn around. Look at me. Look at me, Billy. Look at me. He's telling me to throw my right and the bell rings. The stool's moving so I stand.

He's in front of me and I put up my hands. He punches my body, my arms, my shoulder and I see his chest where his heart's pumping. I wait. It's easier to breathe and I move from the ropes and he follows me, punches, misses, punches, hits and I move away, look for Billy, Look at me and the pull, it's growing, and I hold it and wait. He comes forward, his chest pumping where his heart is, that close and the pull's spreading and he pulls back his arm and his glove starts to move and I'm under and everything, everything, me, my pull, my body, my right hand, I let it go to the place his head should be. The jolt flashes. Knuckles to forearm. No one's in front of me and I need to let it go. The referee's pushing me away and I need to let it go and he's counting. The fighter's trying to stand and stands and the referee stops counting and rubs the fighter's gloves and moves away and the fighter's there, hands down, stepping backward to the ropes and I'm there hitting, hitting, everything. The referee shoves me. The referee's kneeling over the fighter and I'm breathing hard.

I hear voices but nothing specific. I feel my hand

raised. I know I've done something right. I hear someone saying Look at me, Look at me and it's me. The old man walks to me. He opens something and puts it under my nose and it burns and makes me jerk my head. He takes out my mouthpiece. I spit blood on the canvas. He takes my arm and leads me through the ropes and through the people and I smell the dressing room. He sits me in a chair. I want to lie down. I want to close my eyes and rest but the old man won't let me. He makes me sit up and takes off my gloves and cuts my wraps and then goes to another fighter and leads him out of the dressing room.

I sit. I know I've won. My body is heavy. I want to lie down.

Billy comes into the dressing room. He doesn't say anything.

I take off my shoes and socks. I take off my shorts and protector. I shower. The water wakes me. I'm replaying the fight, the parts I remember. I look at my right hand. My knuckles are red and swollen. I press my hands the way the old man pressed them, but it doesn't feel the same. I dress and Billy packs my bag and we don't say anything. We leave the dressing room and walk down the hall and I hear the crowd.

Billy stops walking. "What the fuck?"

He's looking at me and I'm looking at him and I'm so tired and I take Billy and put him against the wall and tell him this is what we have to watch every time, this is what we have to fucking watch and we don't want to watch anymore. I tell him to look at me and look at himself and look at his eyes. I tell him to come back with me but not to fight, back to New York but not to fight, no more fucking fights. I'm holding on to him and my legs are heavy and my arms and he's letting me press him against the wall and Billy's saying All right, all right, all right and I know he's letting me press him against the wall and he's holding me up saying All right. I tell him this is what we have to watch and he says All right.

We leave the arena. We take the metro to the Latin Quarter. Billy walks me to the hotel. He tells me he has to fight once more, he signed a contract to fight, but then he'll go back to New York. He says there's really nothing here for him anyway.

"Get some sleep," Billy says. "You'll be sore tomorrow."

"I'm sore now."

"You'll be more sore tomorrow. Believe me. You'll hurt places you didn't know you had."

I go up to the room. I sit on the mattress. It's quiet. The two fighters tacked to the wall still hold each other.

"Look at me."

My face heals. Four weeks of Paris food and wine and sun put the fight away like a dream.

I sit alone in the arena and wait for Billy. I'm part of the crowd, but it's different this time. A man touches my shoulder, tells me in English I fought well. I say Merci. I've been saying Merci a lot so I just say it. Merci. Bonjour. Bon nuit. He touches my arm and says Dur. Hard. He doesn't know how quickly I was hurt. Or remember. With time it doesn't even matter. I won the fight. It's more recognition than I get for any off-off show. The curtain call ends and I'm back on the street, another New Yorker, the city that big.

Billy enters the ring. Look at you. Look at me. A fighter from Aulnay-sous-Bois, all the nice-sounding names, stands in the blue corner where I stood, the old man behind him. I remember the man's hands on mine.

The fight is ugly. The scar tissue above Billy's eye splits open in the third. He can't get his punches off. He can't see through the blood. The corner men work furiously between rounds, cleaning the cut, applying adrenaline, pressing the enswell against his cheekbones. Billy stalks the French fighter around the ring, punching, punching. I feel what he has to do in my arms. In the fifth round Billy knocks the man down. He walks to the neutral corner and wipes his eye. The Frenchman gets up and the fight goes on.

Billy wins by decision. The referee raises Billy's hand. If she were here and if it weren't Billy's blood, she'd photograph the canvas, the different designs of blood, red smeared by shoes in streaks, red spattered in dots like from flicks of a brush, red diluted by sweat.

I go with Billy to collect his money. It's enough to buy two plane tickets back to New York. Habib wishes us good luck. He says Only in America and laughs.

Billy takes me out for bouillabaisse, then goes off to spend the day with the French woman. He wants to visit the top of the Eiffel Tower just to say he did.

For the rest of the day and night I walk around Paris.

I'm awake when the alarm goes off. I pack my few things. I rip the George Bellows print from the wall and throw it away.

I meet Billy at his hotel. The equipment bag he puts over his shoulder is the same bag he brought to Smythe House.

We take a taxi to the airport.

The 747 takes off on time, non-stop to New York, daylight to daylight, and France disappears behind us.

It's a celebration for Billy, a forced retirement dinner at a place with painted windmills on the walls. We each have three-pound lobsters with green sauce and ice-cold bottled beers and it's the first time Billy's had more than a drink in years and his face is red not from punches. Billy cracks a claw for Sam and Sam orders another round of beers. Billy's laughing and Sam smiles, then throws me a look not to get distant, not now. She wants Billy to feel everything's fine. Billy's telling her about Paris and Habib and about my fight and how I knocked this French kid down with one of the best rights he's ever seen.

"You actually fought," she says.

"He didn't just fight," Billy says. "He killed it. He finished the show."

Billy gets up, says the beer's gone through him, says the day feels like forever, like this morning at the airport was two days ago. I watch him walk through the restaurant to the bathroom in back.

"You could have ruined your face," Sam says. "That would have helped your career."

"It's not ruined, is it?"

"No."

"So it doesn't matter. I brought him back."

"Yes you did. I wish you'd pretend you were happy

about it."

"Is there anything else you'd like me to pretend?"

The waiter sets down three bottles of beer. Another waiter walks by carrying pots of paella. Behind the bar, long, crowded, the bartender mixes pitchers of sangria, ice first, fruit, wine.

"Billy looks happy," she says.

"He's a good liar. And he's drunk."

"Maybe he's not lying. He did come back."

"It was a high."

"You're talking about your fight."

"Even if I'd lost, even if I'd been cut, when I was in there I was alive."

"I'm glad you enjoyed yourself. I hope you didn't tell him that."

"I didn't tell him anything."

"Good."

"I went in there thinking I'd show him something, but maybe all he saw was the high. Winner. The ring's the only place they say it that simply. And the winner is."

"What exactly did you win?" she says.

"I won."

"And?"

"And I won. Just like Billy."

Sam picks up her lobster tail, inspects it, puts it down. She picks up her beer bottle and drinks. She's as tan as I am. She must have taken some days off while we were gone.

"You did a good thing," she says. "That's what I wanted to say. Maybe you even saved him from getting badly hurt."

"Savior of the day."

"You went to France and now you're going to mock it?"

"I don't know why I went."

"You went for him."

"Didn't you tell me I liked seeing him bleed?"

"I was just talking."

"You never just talk. Maybe I didn't mind his blood so much. Maybe I needed to leave for me."

"You hated seeing him hurt."

"I loved seeing him win."

Billy comes back from the bathroom and slides into the booth next to Sam. He puts his arm around her. "This is great. It's great to be back. It's great to see you."

"It's great to see you too," she says.

Billy wants to keep going. We leave the restaurant, go to a bar, order beers, go to another bar, dark, stale-smelling, a line-up of real drinkers, worn pants stuck to barstools. Billy's telling Sam how I threw him against the wall after the fight and it's not his moment to tell. The bartender works slowly, refilling drinks without being asked, first pouring the vodka or gin or whiskey into a shot glass so no one thinks they're getting shorted. One stool over an old man stares at his whiskey. His hands are delicate and too white like he's never been in the sun. Billy's talking about his first fight in Paris, outweighed by fifteen pounds, and the man lifts his head and stares at Billy and says he looks familiar. Billy says he fought twice at the Garden. The old man says he's been going to fights at the Garden for years, to the new Garden, to the old Garden, and if there'd been a middle Garden he'd have gone to that one too. He says how much the game has changed. Sam holds her beer with both hands. She listens to Billy talking about the fights, about hanging up the gloves, about moving on, listening for lies. The old man stops talking and Billy stops talking. Sam puts her hand on Billy's shoulder. She tries to bring him back and Billy says he's not sure what he'll do now and she tells him not to worry, the big decisions just come and I'm listening for her lie. Sam says we should go somewhere else. The old man says he's also hung up his gloves. His hands are on his lap and he tilts his head forward and touches his lips to the glass.

We walk to the Village to drink. We walk to Soho. The bar's new. The music's loud. Abstract paintings burst color. I order three scotches on the rocks. A man comes over to Sam and she knows him from somewhere and I hand her her drink and they're talking about a show at Mary Boone and she's smiling her ambitious smile. I can't get drunk. I can't get drunk happy. Billy's hands are on the bar, the empty rocks glass between them, and he slides closer and his weight presses my arm.

"She looks great, doesn't she?"

"She does."

He tells me I'm a great friend. Going to Paris. Fighting a fight. Billy orders two more drinks. His glazed eyes, stitches above, aren't happy anymore. He asks who the guy is talking to Sam. I tell him I don't know.

"Fuck it," Billy says.

He raises his glass. "Right on time," he says and downs it.

Sam comes back. Billy buys her a drink and we stay at the bar, but the night's over. We're all trying to push something away, but it won't go. The bar empties and the man says good-bye to Sam and Billy's watching him.

We leave the bar.

"What now?" Billy says.

"I have to work tomorrow," Sam says.

"Take the day off."

"I can't. The show's in less than a month."

"One more," he says. "One more for the road. Let's get one more."

"I have to sleep."

We're at the corner. Sam lifts her hand and a taxi slows, stops.

I watch them hug each other. I see her hands on his back. Sam tells Billy she's happy he's back and he'll figure something out and I'm listening for the lie and she knows it. Billy opens the door and Sam gets into the cab.

"New York City," he says. "Back in the Big Apple."

Billy closes the door and the cab drives away.

"I'm drunk," he says.

"It's good for you."

"We were in France this morning. Can you believe it? We were in fucking France. We should be jet-lagged. It feels longer than that."

"It does."

"I'm hungry," Billy says.

"We can find a diner."

"I'm drunk."

We walk west.

"They couldn't pronounce it," he says. "Amburger.

That's how they said it. Amburger. Without the h."

"There's a place open on Sixth Avenue."

"And they didn't taste the same. They didn't sound the same and they didn't taste the same."

Billy laughs.

Pigeons wake me. My head hurts and my mouth is dry. I go to the bathroom to brush my teeth and the room's strange and the toothbrush is hard.

I stand.
They draw.
The instructor tells me to change position.
I do.

Across the car a woman sits with her son. The subway's hot and the kid's hair sticks against his forehead. He's talking away in Spanish and the woman, tired moons under her eyes, nods occasionally to the child but says nothing. There are two full grocery bags at her feet and she holds the handles tight in her hands for no reason.

The kid stands and walks over to one of the car's center poles and starts to climb. When he reaches the top he slides down until he's sitting on the floor. He looks up at the people around him with up-to-something eyes, then stays looking at me.

"Hey, you, what's your name?" the kid says.

"Hey, you, what's your name?" I say

"Hey, you, what's your name?" the kid says, grinning.

"I asked you first."

"No you didn't."

"What's the question?"

The kid thinks a second. "What's your name?" he says.

"What's yours?"

"I'm not telling," he says. "What's your name?"

"You're very persistent."

"What's that?"

"You keep trying without giving up."

The kid laughs, jumps up and climbs the center pole again. "I bet you can't do this," he says.

The woman yells something in Spanish. The kid's mouth gets serious and he slides down the pole and sits back down next to his mother. She stays staring ahead, her hands on the bags.

I get off at 86th Street and walk east. It's a callback for an independent film and independent films sometimes hit big, actors in independent films sometimes get found, stories of movie stars all going back to something, one thing, a beginning where, in retrospect, odds seem possible. As soon I got back, not to think, I started the routine. I bought *Backstage* and circled listings for independent films, student films, showcases, anything with a part I might fit. I went to auditions, handed over my picture and resumé, did my monologue or read sides for the director in front of me or the small camera set on a tripod. And when I walked back through the waiting room, done, and saw all the actors waiting their turn, the ones who looked like they'd been leads in high school musicals, the ones talking too loud about working with famous actors when all they'd done was extra work, the ones practicing their monologues with moving lips before they did them for real, the ones pretending they were already stars, I didn't want it. I'd already stopped doing movie-star moves in the mirror.

I don't recognize the few actors sitting in the hall from the first audition and the proctor's new. His hair's very gray and he wears glasses halfway down his nose and his eyes look over his glasses, looking, it seems, at nothing, a gaze the opposite of dreams. I tell the proctor I have a two o'clock appointment. His eyes shift down and he puts a check next to my name and gives me sides to read. Chairs line the hall wall. I sit at the end of the row.

The scene's between a young man and his father so I look at the proctor and pretend he's my father, pretend these are my lines and I'm talking to him, his empty eyes not recognizing me, no different than if I met my real one if he's still around, if we could recognize each other, which we couldn't. The actor two chairs over breathes heavy like he wants me to look, breathes heavy again, emoting frustration.

"It's been cast," he says.

If his face filled a screen it would be bland, not worth watching, no chance of making it. I could tell him. I could tell him to go home, start something new, maybe get out of the city before he becomes a lifelong extra or a lifelong waiter or a proctor with dead eyes, but I've told enough. He presses his lips and shakes his head, exaggerating the motion, performing disgust.

"I'm serious," he says. "The part's already cast."

"How do you know?"

"My friend was temping at CAA last week and he overheard some agents talking about an indie film that signed someone big. It turns out it's this one. My friend's not sure which actor, but someone with a name."

"They should have told us."

"It looks bad to the union if they cancel auditions. At least we got called back."

"Called back for nothing."

"They're probably still casting the smaller parts, so I figured I'd read. You know how it is. You read for something, you get something else. That's why I'm here. It's still annoying though."

The actor shakes his head, stands, walks to the corner of the room, looks at his sides, mouths the words. He's making all kinds of faces.

It's a circle. Open auditions held but casting closed. Closed auditions inaccessible but casting open. Just getting into the Screen Actors Guild, SAG, three letters on a coveted membership card, the first step to nine letters spread across a mountain, HOLLYWOOD in giant white capitals, is a circle. To get a union card you have to be in a union film. To be in a union film you have to have a union card. There are ways to break this circle, ways every actor knows, which take time, which cost money, which don't get you into closed auditions. I paid to join the television union, finally received an under-five on a soap, spoke a single line as I walked behind the leads, which made me eligible to join SAG, which made me eligible to pay yearly dues, which entitles me to audition for parts already cast. I look at the sides, look at the words, just words, just a proctor, not my father.

The actor goes in. The actor comes out. The proctor calls my name. I walk into the room. Director, producer, writer sitting behind the table, same as the first audition, all business, like they're really looking for an actor. Same cameraman behind the camera. And someone I haven't seen, a middle-aged man sitting in a chair with sides in his hands. There's an empty chair next to him where I'm supposed to sit, his son.

"All set?" the director says.

"Are you?"

"Ready when you are."

"I heard a rumor the part's already cast."

"Thanks for sharing."

"Is it true?"

"Are you ready to read?" the director says.

"I'm asking you a question. I'd like to know where I stand."

The director looks at the man next to him, the producer, who gives nothing. The director looks back at me.

"We have a lot of people to see today. Are you ready to read?"

"That's why I'm here. But I want to know if the part's already cast."

"Do you want to read or do you want to argue?" the producer says.

"I want to know."

The producer taps his watch.

"You are wasting time," he says, enunciating wasting, taking precious seconds stretching out the words.

"I spent a day at the open audition. I spent a half hour on the subway getting here. I've been waiting in the hall. I have two minutes to prove myself for a part you might have already cast. Don't tell me about wasting time."

"I think you should leave now," the director says.

"I should do a lot of things."

"Please go. You're not someone I'll ever work with."

I sit in the chair and face the actor playing the father. He has the first line in the scene.

"We want you to leave," the producer says

"I'm going to read."

"No you're not. You're going to leave the premises."

"The premises? Are you trying to sound like a cop? Is that part of your job besides putting up money?"

"My job doesn't concern you."

"It does concern me. I'm looking for a job and you're the man with the checkbook."

"Listen, you insolent punk. You're done here. Time's up."

"Not yet."

I look at the actor.

"Go on," I say.

The actor looks toward the table. He doesn't say his first line.

I read my line, pause where the father's supposed to talk, read my next line, pause, read my next line. It's easy to do. I didn't have a father to fill in the lines anyway. I go through the whole scene, line by line, pausing where I should be listening. I say my last line, lower my head like the character is saying good-bye, raise my head like I'm back. I look at the three people behind the table. The woman, the writer, the one who hasn't said a word, nods her head so no one but me can see.

"Now you can leave," the director says.

"You should know better," I say to the woman.

"Why should I know better?"

"You're not like them."

"You're right," she says.

"I just wanted to act."

"That was good."

"But maybe I just wanted to be a movie star."

I look at the director and the producer. I've seen exaggerated faces, exaggerated gestures, heard exaggerated words since I got here. So I pull my finger across my throat.

"See you on the street," I say.

"Is that a threat?" the producer says.

"Time's up."

"If you don't leave immediately, I'm calling the police." His face is red. His hand's on his phone.

"Call them. Call them to the premises. Put out a fucking APB. All points just for me."

I look at the actor not playing my father.

"Good job," I say.

I stand and walk over to the table. I move my hand fast and the director and producer flinch. I put the sides face down.

I walk out of the audition room. The proctor looks at me like he can't recall if he's seen me before, then his eyes go down, not from shame, but to look through his glasses, and he calls the next name on the list.

Sparring in all three rings, trainers calling out combinations, fists hitting heavy bags, fists hitting speed bags making the rhythm for the room, Gleason's Gym, and the smell of sweat and exhaustion.

I wrap my hands, put on gloves, walk to the heavy bags. One bag's free and I hit it once to feel the pressure against my knuckles. I start working the bag. Jabs and hooks and straight rights. The bag keeps coming, quivering on its chains.

The buzzer rings. I stop punching. My breathing slows. Phil Brice comes over and smiles kind. His stomach's big and his legs are bad, but I've seen him throw punches, demonstrating combinations for his fighters, and his hands are still fast and he's still solid under his bright Hawaiian shirt. Phil says he heard Billy fought in France and I tell him he won twice and now he's back in the city. He asks how Billy's doing without asking about his eyes. I haven't seen Billy since we drank. I tell him Billy's fine. He asks how I'm doing and I tell him I'm here for the exercise.

"It's a good feeling," Phil says. "After a good workout you feel you can take the world. You pull off your gloves and unwrap your hands and you're that fast and strong. Tell Billy I said hello."

Phil walks across the gym to work with a fighter in the center ring. I hit the bag. I jump rope. I'm not in Paris shape, but I feel good.

I leave Gleason's and walk past the loading dock steps where I'd sit and wait for Billy to shower after I watched him spar. When he came out of the gym, bag over his shoulder, he always looked calm, the sweet side of exhaustion. Between the warehouses I see a piece of Brooklyn Bridge, cables spreading symmetrically, reflecting light. There's a breeze off the river and my knuckles are skinned and it's coolest where it's almost bleeding like that one less layer of skin makes a difference.

Billy calls. He says he has to see me. I ask what's wrong, but he says we should meet, says he can come to my place or I can come to his or we can meet in Washington Square. I say I'll be at the arch in an hour.

It's hot, the kind of hot that makes pavement soft. The streets are quiet and even the cars driving down Seventh Avenue look sluggish. The park is quiet too. A few students sit in the concrete circle around the fountain, some talking, some reading, some just watching water shoot into air. Two dogs in the dog run stand still.

I see Billy. He waves once. His shoulders roll the way they roll in the ring when he presses forward, always forward, even when Antwan Davis had him hurt, moving forward until the end. His T-shirt says Lonsdale Boxing with two gloves underneath.

"Hot," he says.

"It is."

"Run in this you'll drop five pounds. I haven't run once since we got back. You miss Paris?"

"I don't know."

"You ever think about getting out of this city?"

"I think about it."

"Sometimes I feel like we're stuck here. We used to talk so much about coming to New York and making it and now it's like we can't leave, just because we put so much into being here. Then again, we haven't been here that long."

His nose somehow flatter, his ears thicker, the lines of scar tissue cut into his brows show how long.

"I've got something to tell you you're not going to like," he says.

He's keeping his eyes on my eyes, and I know him, know he's forcing himself to keep his eyes steady.

"I slept with Sam."

It spreads from my throat down.

It spreads and presses and I slit my eyes, try forcing it away.

And I'm thinking the punch you don't see is the punch that knocks you out, a boxing line, an easy boxing line, that's what I'm thinking and I'm slitting my eyes, forcing it away.

"I got a job working the door at a bar. I was getting home late and waking too early like I had roadwork to do. I wasn't sleeping right. I'd catch a subway to Gleason's and stand outside listening to the gym. I even booked a flight back to France and then cancelled it. I hated the job. All I did was stand there checking IDs. The night I quit she called to see how I was. We met for a drink and it happened."

His hands are down, his face is open and I stay on his eyes.

"You broke the rules."

"What rules?" Billy says.

"You broke them."

My voice almost breaks. I force myself to swallow.

"We're not at Smythe House," Billy says and then he moves his eyes. "I didn't mean for it to happen. But it happened. I'm sorry."

"Nothing just happens with Sam."

"Don't tell me you never wanted her."

"You're weak."

"Then so is Sam. Everybody's weak except for you."

"I should knock you out."

Billy's eyes go hard. "Take your shot."

"You fucked up."

"We all fucked up. You should have left me in France."

"You're blaming me? What are you, a fucking child?"

Billy's eyes are hard and hurt too and I know all the ways his eyes can go and she knows all the ways and his hands are down and I ask if he feels better now that he's fucking Sam and he tells me to fuck off and I ask if he fucking feels better now and he says he only slept with her once and it's in my throat, the weight pressing down.

"I'm sorry," he says.

I swallow.

I force myself to breathe. I hear Billy breathing. The pressing's still there and I swallow again.

"The big decisions just come," I say. "When I went to France, I didn't know what I was going to do. Then I did. Then I just did. That's what she told you. The big decisions just come."

"That's what she told me."

"I'd get in the ring. That was the big decision. I'd fight one fight so you could see what it's like watching your friend get hurt."

"Now I know what it's like," Billy says.

"Do you?"

"I know what that's like. That's boxing. It's part of the game."

"It's part of the game. Your exact words. When we went to the hospital. When the fighter died. I didn't show you anything."

Billy steps forward, just a step, but it feels like more, like he's rolling forward. "You landed a lucky shot against a French kid who didn't even know how to throw a punch. You thought that would show me something?"

"Don't turn this around."

"Standing there in the ring saying *Look at me*. Screaming *Look at me*. What can you show me?"

"Nothing."

His shoulders are closer. "What can you show me?"

"Say it again. You don't scare me."

"What can you show me? I see people getting hurt while I'm hurting them. You think I'm stupid? You felt sorry for me or something? Because I lost two fights you felt sorry for me? Is that why you and Sam decided you should go over to France?"

"It was me who went over. It was my idea."

"She said you both talked about it."

"I told her I was going."

"I was beating grown men at eleven years old. I broke my father's fucking jaw when I was eleven years old. After that it was just me. You know how it goes. We all know how it goes. Wherever the state put me, it was just me and nobody really gave a shit and in no time at all I knew I didn't need anything from anyone. You should have remembered that before you got on the plane."

Billy's hands are fists. The muscles in his jaw are tight like he's biting down. I look past Billy. At the park. At the few people. At how the heat dulls the light.

"You think Sam feels sorry for me?" Billy says.

"I don't think anything anymore."

"Tell me if you think so. You think I slept with Sam because I couldn't deal with anything and she slept with me because she felt sorry for me?"

"I don't know why you fucked."

"I don't believe this," Billy says.

"Is that how you do it?"

"Do what?"

"Counterpunch. Is that how you turn it around?"

I hear him breathe. "No. You're right," he says.

"It was the three of us. Even if things are different here, it was the three of us. Didn't you know this would change something forever?"

He's forcing his eyes to stay on mine and then the forcing goes away.

"It already changed," he says.

"It did," he says. "You know it did. It already changed."

His voice is quiet and he relaxes his hands.

A dog in the dog run barks once. There's no threat in it, only habit on a too-hot day.

"There's something else you should know," Billy says. "I'm in love with her."

I take it. Take it and touch it. Touch it the way I've seen cut men touch a cut. The way they open the flesh with their fingers to wipe the blood before they try to stop the bleeding. "I'd never tell her," he says. "Just like you'd never tell her. I've seen you watch her. You've seen me watch her and I've seen you. It's no surprise."

He's not forcing his eyes anywhere anymore.

"What?" he says. "You going to disown us?"

"It happened," he says.

"*All the talk that went across these two beds, huh? Our whole lives. Yeah. Lotta dreams and plans.*"

"What's that?"

"Some lines from a monologue I used to do."

Billy's standing still. Then he throws a punch at nothing. His fist makes a sound a woodwind might make if it were thrown across an empty room and then he puts his hand down and looks at me.

The strain of a garbage truck's compactor opens another city morning. Next to me the woman breathes heavy. I listen to cars speeding on the empty avenue that's like a highway in the dark and make a deal. If I can hold my breath until ten cars pass I won't care and won't think and it's stupid but I hold my breath anyway and wait.

When the tenth car passes I get up, pick my clothes off the floor, go into the bathroom, the light flickers then settles, squeeze toothpaste on my finger, rub it against my teeth, wintergreen, and dress.

There are pictures in the living room of parents, probably, of brothers and sisters and friends in places outside the city, smiling faces against different backgrounds, a docked sailboat, a snow-covered mountain with ski lifts, a beach so clean it's like a set, white sand and palms. I leave the apartment.

Central Park is two avenues away. The street slopes up then down into trees silhouetted by the just-lit sky. I walk to the park and along the park and downtown. The row of office buildings on the Avenue of the Americas looks deserted. The statues in front of Credit Lyonnais, female figures without heads or arms, remind me of France and the *Winged Victory* and I sat on the Louvre's steps and thought of her. The buildings become smaller. The light lighter. Twenty blocks a mile. I've walked four miles. People are out. I buy a container of orange juice and on the wall behind the register hang headshots of the greats. Ali. Holmes. Duran. Hagler. Chavez. Whitaker. Fighters everywhere.

I keep walking.

"Excuse me. May I talk to you for a moment?"

He's in good shape but older. His eyes look kind.

"What?"

"I noticed you walking," he says.

I'm ready to tell him thanks for the compliment, but I'm not interested. It's what I always say these days.

"Are you a dancer?" he says.

"A dancer?"

"Do you dance? You're built like a dancer."

"I don't dance."

"Are you an artist of some sort?"

"Not today."

"I thought you were a dancer," the man says. "The reason I'm asking is because we're having a meeting this evening. For artists, mostly dancers, but many of them are students if that's what you are. Are you religious at all?"

"What do you want?"

"We pray together and ask Jesus to support us in whatever we're doing. It's very informal. There's no priest or anything like that. It's more of a communal service. We read a little scripture and sometimes the artists perform something for the meeting. I think you'd like it. Really, there are no strings."

"You believe that?"

He looks away, doubt, tolerance, I'm not sure, then back, his eyes still kind.

"I run the meetings and they're very informal," he says. "It's a very communal spiritual experience."

"Maybe when I take up dance."

"I really thought you were a dancer, but it's fine if you're not. Here's our card. The address is where we hold our eight o'clock meetings. There are even refreshments."

"Refreshments?"

"Yes."

"Why didn't you say so?"

"We have juice and cookies."

"Orange juice?"

"Orange. Usually apple."

"I'm kidding."

"Well, I hope you'll come. God be with you."

The man walks away. His posture is excellent.

I stand.
They draw.
Billy calls.
Sam calls.
I don't answer.
The instructor tells me to change position.
I do.

The Port Authority is Sunday-morning empty. I've gone to the gym every day for two weeks, worked for ten rounds, twelve rounds, twelve hard rounds, sometimes more, hitting the bags, hitting the mitts when Phil Brice calls me into the ring, shadowboxing in the long mirrors until my arms are heavy, jumping rope to the buzzer, past the buzzer, jumping until I trip. And in my room I keep the shade up all the way so the sun wakes me, so I can run to Central Park and back and sleep before taking the A train to Gleason's.

I walk through the station, gym bag over my shoulder. I buy a ticket to Atlantic City and wait in line.

The bus pulls in. The people getting off look tired under the station's fluorescent light. I hand the driver my ticket and sit near the back.

The bus moves quickly through the Lincoln Tunnel. From the Jersey side of the Hudson, the Empire State Building separates the skyline into two parts and the city's still clear, no smog pushing down yet, blurring the lines and edges and angles. There's a line-up of planes coming into Newark Airport, spaced safely apart, a light on each wing, landing so slow they should fall. I close my eyes and make the highway bumps turbulence and it's almost like flying.

I'm restless. Garden State Parkway. Atlantic City Expressway. The trip's longer than I thought. Trees separate.

Land flattens. It looks like coast.

The bus turns into Atlantic City and stops at a long light and along the avenue it's every famous store, every familiar logo, and a few blocks down the newest casinos, all glass, look like offices. The bus takes a hard left away from the stores, drives to the station, parks, idles. I get off and find the bathroom. My piss is clear, scared piss.

I check the gym's address. The back streets aren't the front streets. Abandoned buildings, cracked lots, houses tilted by abuse, old bars with neon signs, beer names, faded reds and blues, faded greens that give off sad light. A metal sign bolted to the gym's door says it opens at ten. I switch my bag to my other shoulder and walk to the Boardwalk, take off my shoes, walk on the beach, sand morning-cool, no one around. I undress behind a cement pillar from an old pier and hang my bag over a piece of rebar. I run to the ocean and dive in and swim past the swell and feel the strength of the water and my own strength and I'll need my strength and I turn, swim back, sit on the sand. I know what it will be like this time and I lie back and close my eyes and let the orange spread and the red.

I get up and dress.

I stretch my muscles until they burn. A seagull approaches, its face ugly up close, and I clap to make it fly. I walk back to the boardwalk and through the streets. The gym's open.

It's easy to recognize the fighter in red shorts moving around the ring, throwing jabs and hooks, slipping imaginary punches, circling, circling. He's completely focused. His mouth is closed, hardly breathing. He pivots off his left foot and moves forward, snapping combinations, three punches, four punches, the way he did when he beat Billy Carlyle and when he beat him again.

I wait for Antwan Davis to finish shadow boxing. The buzzer rings. He takes a towel off the top rope and wipes sweat from his face. He looks down at me from the raised ring.

"What you want?" he says.

"I have a favor to ask."

"A favor? I got no money."

"I was hoping we could spar a few rounds."

"I already got sparring partners."

"Just a few rounds. That's all I'm asking."

"A few rounds of me taking it easy. You ever fought?"

"Once."

"You win?"

"I won."

Antwan Davis wipes the back of his neck and puts the towel over the top rope.

"You know that don't mean shit," he says.

"I know."

"Winning one fight, being undefeated after one fight, that shit's nothing. That's one fight is all that is."

"Can we spar?"

"Why you got to spar me?"

"You're undefeated."

Antwan Davis smiles. "That's correct. Difference is, I got twenty wins next to my undefeated. You looking to break my streak?"

"I saw you fight a couple times. I thought you could help me learn some things."

"You want to go to work."

"I want to go to work."

Antwan Davis throws a combination at the air so fast I can't count the punches, then leans over the rope, no smile in his mouth or eyes.

"One win. You want to put your one against my twenty and see what you got. You got shoes and shit in your bag?"

"I do."

"Go change in back. I'll give you three rounds. Be quick. My trainer coming soon and he don't like me sparring when he not here."

"Thank you."

"Don't thank me until you done. You might not be thanking me then."

I go back, change, put on the cheap pair of boxing shoes I wore in France, lucky shot, Billy's words, and I control it, control it, wrap my hands, roll my neck, stretch my arms, my shoulders.

Antwan Davis is talking to a thickly-muscled man with an ex-fighter's face. I walk over. The man introduces himself as Mr. Joe, the owner of the gym. His eyes are brown and bloodshot. He says he'll get me some headgear and gloves and a protective cup for my manhood and he smirks and walks to his office.

"Where you from?" Antwan says.

"I live in New York."

"You fought in New York?"

"I fought in Paris."

"What the fuck you go all the way there for?"

"I don't know."

"The man wanted to charge you for being here, but I told him you going to pay enough. Lesson's on me."

"I'll thank you after."

Antwan stretches. Mr. Joe returns. I step into the protector and he helps me on with the gloves, rubs Vaseline over my face, buckles the headgear under my chin, puts in my mouthpiece. I press my teeth down until it hurts. He goes to Antwan Davis. The last time I saw him he was standing near the exit, the winner, and Billy came out of the dressing room and Sam wanted to go. The pressing's not there, throat-pressing, I've moved it away, and fuck them.

I climb into the ring. It's not loud, no lights in my eyes, no crowd. All I see are gym walls and Antwan Davis standing across from me, relaxed and easy and still unmarked, and Mr. Joe in the middle of the ring looking me over.

"You ready?" he says.

"Ready." The mouthpiece thickens my word.

He waits for the ring buzzer. It rings.

"Let's get it on," he says, a mock announcer, and laughs.

Antwan walks to me and I hear my shoes rubbing against canvas, the hollow whistle of air in my headgear. He jabs, jabs again, fast, faster than I thought a man could punch. I have to concentrate completely on every second. I have to keep my hands high, move my head. His eyes are clear, but now there's no expression in them. They're the eyes Billy told me about. He said they never blinked. A jab hits the top of my headgear. A jab hits my chin. I tuck my head, step forward, throw my right, miss. I bounce my feet against the canvas hoping for some rhythm.

"Go to work," Antwan says through his mouthpiece.

I adjust my headgear. I move in, jab, and he's under my arm and his uppercut snaps my chin, jams my mouthpiece. I taste blood. He cut Billy and he's cut me and I wipe my mouth and Mr. Joe's watching and I move forward, punch, miss, punch, miss, his jab hits me, stops me. I step back and keep my eyes on his eyes and I'm breathing heavy. I need to start fighting and he hits my face. I need to feel the pull and he hits my face. I lift my hands higher. I watch Antwan's eyes. I try to slow time. Antwan jabs my head, my chest, circling, circling and I can't get in and he jabs, jabs, jabs and there's nothing I can do and I'm the only one to do it and he hooks my body and my breath's gone and I step back to breathe and the buzzer rings.

"How the lesson so far?" Antwan says.

I don't say anything.

"You want to keep going?" Mr. Joe says.

"Yes."

I walk to the corner. No one's waiting for me. I lean against the ring post, rest my arms on the ropes, my arms too heavy, try to slow my breaths. I spit blood. I look at Antwan Davis standing across from me. He's hardly breathing. His mouthpiece rests easily in his mouth. I move my feet, one foot forward one foot back one foot forward one foot back, something to do, supposed to do. The buzzer rings.

"Work," Antwan says.

I rush Antwan. He steps aside and smiles over his mouthpiece. I rush him again, throwing punches and he's not there and I pay like Billy paid. He hits too fast, jabs moving my headgear, jabs stinging my mouth. I spit blood. I force myself forward. Antwan's hands are down and he's asking What you learning, what you learning, repeating the words like a dare. He circles, circles, talking. I feint a left, throw the right, feel the punch land. Antwan stops talking. He squares his body. I ready myself to take what he'll give. His punches are slower, sound thicker, all hit me, all hurt. I take it. I force myself to take it. I try to slow his movement, but I can't. I try to reach him, but I can't. I'm not good enough. I know I'm not good enough. I know fighting in this gym means nothing. I knew it. I know it. I'll never beat the man who beat Billy. Billy will never beat this man. I turn my head, spit a chunk of blood on the canvas, swallow another chunk. I see his body turning into the punch. I feel it, hear it, thick, heavy, even as I'm bending over, even as I want to puke, time slowed in the pressing pain, in the not breathing, in my arms covering my stomach, anything to cover my stomach even if he hits my head. I look up and he's right there. His eyes give nothing. I wait and it's slow and I wait. Antwan doesn't punch. He steps back to let me breathe. I try to straighten my body. He pushes me against the ropes and throws punches at my arms, just my arms, and he lets me grab on and I hold him and hold him and the pull won't come and the buzzer rings and Antwan walks back to his corner.

I rest my arms on the ropes. This time no one talks. They don't ask if I want to keep fighting and they don't tell me to quit. The round buzzer rings. My legs are heavy. My arms are heavy. I have nothing. Antwan circles without punching. I focus on standing. He dances the rest of the round, throwing his jab and moving, throwing his jab and moving, and there's nothing I can do.

The buzzer rings. I swallow the blood sliding down my throat. I spit my mouthpiece onto my glove. I suck deep breaths. I thank Antwan Davis. He nods once. He tells me to work on my jab, everything starts with the jab. Mr. Joe helps me off with the gloves. He unbuckles the headgear. I step out of the protective cup. Mr. Joe takes it, taps it with his finger.

"You can shower off in back if you like," he says. "No charge."

I go to the lockers. I take off my shoes and shorts. I shower and rinse the blood from my mouth. I dress. I put my bag over my shoulder.

Antwan is still in the ring, alone, gloves off, moving and moving, beautifully moving, everything fluid, everything clean. I walk to the ring and watch Antwan Davis dance.

The buzzer rings. He stops and comes over. He tells me to work on my jab.

"You ever think about Billy Carlyle?"

"Billy Carlyle. I beat him twice. What I got to think about?"

"How good is he?"

"He can fight."

"Could he get better?"

"He wasn't any better the second time I fought him. He cut too easy. He cut bad both times we fought. Why? You know him?"

"I did."

"Sure. He tough."

I wish Antwan luck. I tell him I hope he'll become champion one day. He says he will, guaranteed, and he moves to the center of the ring and starts to punch. I know the champions in his division. I've seen them fight on television and he'll have a hard time.

Clouds are coming in, but the sky's still clear over the Atlantic. I walk the boardwalk to the Tropicana, cool inside, fresh oxygen to keep players playing. A bathroom attendant's wiping the sink. My piss is back to yellow. I wash my face and rinse my mouth and there's still blood when I spit. There's a bruise under my eye. I need a shave. I want to rest. The attendant gives me a paper towel.

"Rough morning?" he says.

"You should have seen the other guy."

I put a buck in the basket.

I walk through the streets to the bus station. I ask the woman at the information desk when the next bus leaves for New York. I sit and wait and watch.

Before I got to Smythe House I snuck into movies all the time. There was always a side door and I was a fast kid. I loved the cool and the darkness and the going away. In one town the theater was from another time. A billowing gold curtain would open spectacularly, folding in on itself as the light went dark, and there it would be, the big screen, the biggest screen, and the movie would start. Hollywood became my dream. My kid's dream. My look-at-me dream. And I would have gone straight there, but I met Billy and I met Sam and their dreams were in New York and New York was good too.

West Broadway and Broome.

People standing outside the building talking. People standing inside the door waiting for the elevator. I walk the stairs to the second floor and there they are, the colors Sam uses, the blues and blacks and brighter reds, the figures and faces the way she paints, some almost Billy and some almost me. She photographed us at Smythe House and when we first came to New York, usually when we weren't looking, and she painted from her photographs. Sometimes she photographed us, then streaked lines over the pictures, red and black, across face and body. And if the light were perfect she told us to stand in the light. Billy hated standing still, but I didn't. When I quit my third bartending job Sam suggested the Art Students League. I'd stood naked before. It was easy.

The lines of my almost-body look strong and she's got my eyes right or almost right. In one painting my eyes are completely open, maybe how they should be, and I'm looking out and I can even see their color, green, but a lighter green than mine, like something new.

Sam stands in the middle of the room. Her back's to me. Her legs are dark. She's been outside. She's talking to people I don't know.

Three paintings hang on each of the four walls. I get as close to one as I can, not of Billy, not of me, and the canvas is so big it's like I'm in it, all colors and shapes and the outline of a woman I don't recognize. I listen to the couple standing next to me. It's what Billy and I did at her shows at Columbia so we could tell her what people said. I see where the brushstrokes start. I see where the layers of paint are thickest. Sometimes I'd walk by the high school art room and she'd be there alone, working, and I'd watch her through the window.

People are talking to Sam and I move to the next painting, a red dot next to it, already sold.

Billy walks into the gallery. I watch him walk to Sam. I watch him wait for the people around her to leave. I watch him kiss her cheek once. I can't see her face. He talks to her and more people are waiting to talk to her and he walks away. He sees me and comes over.

"You're here," he says.

"I'm here."

"I never saw her again."

I look at the wall behind him. There are two more red dots.

"I tried calling you," he says. "I tried calling you a bunch of times. You never answered your phone."

"I didn't want to talk to you."

"I probably wouldn't want to talk to me either."

Billy moves his eyes and we both look at the people and the people around Sam and the paintings, almost Billy, almost me, and that's what we are, almost, slivers of past things making all three of us off, the off almost not visible but there.

"Lots of red dots," Billy says.

"That's the goal."

"And all these people."

Billy's eyes, always so clear, are tired.

"I knew she'd make it," he says. "I knew we all would."

Make it. Making it. Words repeated so often they became one word, Makingit, too easy to say, like a habit, like a lie. Like the lie he'll win a string of fights without his eyes opening up, a kid with potential and no scars, moving toward a title, a belt. I wonder if he sees the belt when he's lying, if it's real or if it's been glorified into something that doesn't exist, if the jewels are too big, the colors too bright. I wonder if he believes Sam's success is the start of ours, all of us making it, the three of us, one, two, three, falling into place.

"Anyway," Billy says. "I better get going. I need to take a run. I've started running nights instead of mornings. I found a new trainer and he says running nights is going to get my internal clock ready for fight time."

The bartenders pour wine and sparkling water. The people walk around the room.

"Anyway," Billy says.

The word stays there, a word to fill space, a residue of broken rules, sad and awkward and empty, and I keep my eyes slits like walking a runway, making everything out there away.

He puts out his hand. His knuckles are red from the gym.

"Come on," he says. "It doesn't have to mean anything except this."

"Come on," he says again.

I shake his hand.

"Look at all these people," he says. "She really made it."

I watch Billy leave.

I walk to Sam.

I stand behind her.

I put my fingers against her shoulder hard enough to make her move.

She turns. Her eyes open all the way.

"You fucked him."

Sam looks at the people around her and she smiles and asks them to excuse her. She walks through the room and past the elevators and opens the Exit door and I'm behind her, the stairs light gray, the walls white without any marks like they've just been painted. We walk down until the stairs end and she opens the basement door and it's a warehouse, cement floor and cement walls and large boxes and rolls of bubble wrap and overhead rows of too much light.

She stops and I stop an arm's length away.

"I don't blame you for wanting to embarrass me."
Her hands are at her sides, nothing to hold. "I wanted to
talk to you. I wanted to explain something to you even if I
didn't know what to explain. And I wanted it out of my head
before the show. That part is selfish, I know. I didn't imagine
my first show like this, not when I first imagined it."

"You fucked him."

"He was talking like he didn't care. He was talking like
he didn't care if he got hurt and I kept thinking about the
fighter we saw die. He's always there. He's always there when
Billy fights."

"Is he here?"

"What do you mean?"

"How many people did you fuck to get this show?"
Her pupils go from hurt to hard. "I mean all the way back.
To get you from where you were, from where you came
from, to here?"

"You came from the same place," she says.

"How many?"

"That's my business."

"Did you give him that smile of yours?"

"Don't."

"The smile that shows you'll do anything?"

"Fuck you."

"Not easy crazy. You hated when other kids said that.
But our crazy. The kind we didn't tell Billy about. Fucking to
get something."

"I'll tell you what I did," she says and then she breathes.
"I drank until I was sick. The last four fights when he was
hurt and cut and bleeding, I'd go out afterward, after I left
you two, and I'd drink. I'd drink and drink. I'd drink myself
sick to replace the sick I felt seeing him fight."

"That's very dramatic."

"It's not dramatic. It's true."

"The fighter who died. It's the same lie I told myself
when I went to France. You didn't just fuck him for that. It's
not the truth."

"What's the truth?"

"You needed to get something."

"What did I need to get?"

"I understand it's easier without us. Making it. But getting rid of us like that was wrong."

She doesn't move. I hear cars moving but far away. I hear voices but far away, no words. The light's too light. Her face is washed out.

"You know what you did."

"Maybe," she says.

"Just be honest."

"Maybe you're right. Maybe I need to be free. There. I said it. That's what I needed to get."

It's like the quiet afterward. He'd come, folded twenties in my pocket, and all the noise, his hand, his mouth, stopped.

"Now I need to go upstairs," she says. "It's my show. You don't have to believe this, but part of me thought I could save him."

"No one saves anyone."

"I know."

"He started training."

"I know that too."

"He's in love with you, Sam."

Her name, my voice, out loud, Sam, and her pupils go thin then wide.

"No."

"He is. He's in love with you."

I put my hand around her throat. To stop her. Stop the talk.

I feel her hands around my arm, both hands.

I press my head against her head.

Her hands press harder.

I loosen my hand and she breathes in, out, in, then her mouth's against my mouth, breathing into my mouth, her mouth soft then hard, the way it was, one time, one time outside the three of us, one time before I moved her away, my hands on her, her shoulders, her back, her ass, her legs, pushing, pushing her thighs, pushing in my fingers and she's pushing down and I lift her, lift her cunt, take my cock, push through her, fuck her, fuck her, fuck her, her eyes open watching me, me watching her, years of watching, years, her face red, her mouth open, sounds coming from her throat, now and now and I stop.

I take my cock out. I step back. I belt my pants.

"You're free."

She doesn't say anything. She's breathing hard. The light's too light.

I'm on the stairs.

I'm on the street.

I'm running.

According to the program, Jenaro Cruz is an up-and-coming middlcwcight from the Bronx with a big punch and ten consecutive knockouts. Billy Carlyle is a hard hitter whose only two losses came at the hands of Antwan Davis. The program states this is Billy's first fight back in New York after two fights in Paris.

It's still early. People are coming in. The bell rings and the two lightweights stop punching and return to their corners. The referee leans against the ropes. Antwan Davis, wearing his red track suit, walks through the crowd. The bell rings and the lightweights come out of their corners. They stay busy and finish the round throwing. The decision's announced.

Two new fighters enter the ring, one with Phil Brice, his Hawaiian shirt orange and ocean blue, surfboards on cartoon waves. Phil Brice's fighter throws well-schooled combinations. The ring girls circle between rounds. A kid asks Antwan Davis for an autograph. Phil Brice's fighter knocks out his opponent.

Fighters not fighting are called into the ring. Antwan Davis steps forward when his name's announced, lifts both arms. The announcer tells the crowd Antwan's now ranked in the top ten in the middleweight division.

The seats are almost full. The house lights are turned

down. The blue canvas brightens under the overhead lights. Bass beats echo. I don't recognize the man in front of Billy, but I see Billy in his white robe with his name in light blue across the back. The hood of his robe covers his head. He walks slowly to the ring and the man opens the ropes and Billy steps through and starts pacing the canvas.

The other fighter walks to the ring. His robe is blue with red letters and he also wears his hood. He steps through the ropes and his handlers remove his robe. Jenaro Cruz is thick, thick arms, thick shoulders, thick thighs and calves. His back is as wide as Billy Carlyle's. The two fighters move around the ring without looking at each other. The announcer introduces them and gives their records and they walk to the center of the ring and the referee gives final instructions. Both fighters look at the floor, nod their heads, touch gloves and return to their corners.

Billy looks straight ahead. He moves one foot forward, one foot back, one foot forward, one foot back. He waits for the bell to ring to move forward to hurt the man in front of him. Jenaro Cruz also looks ready. The fear's controlled in each fighter's eyes. The referee points to the timekeeper, the bell rings and Billy doesn't have to wait anymore.

I watch. I don't yell for him to jab between Cruz's arms to get to his heart. I don't yell for him to throw a right over Cruz's left to get to his head. I watch the two fighters press into each other and punch each other in the middle of the ring. It's not that hard to watch. Heads snap. Bodies bend. Rounds go by. And then Billy steps back and wipes his eye and the blood's started. When the bell rings blood smears Billy's face and shoulders and chest.

The cut man spreads Billy's cut and applies adrenaline. I went to France to bring Billy back and he's back.

The bell rings, Billy moves forward, Cruz jabs and the cut starts bleeding. I watch them punch. I watch them hold. I watch them move around the ring attached and I watch them move around the ring with distance between them. I watch the blood flow. Cruz is swinging wildly now, energized every time his gloves hit flesh or muscle. Billy keeps blinking, keeps wiping his eye, keeps moving forward. Cruz pivots and throws a right that's amateur wide, traveling so much distance it's like a movie punch, and I watch it connect against Billy's jaw. His head snaps. His legs buckle. The crowd stands. I don't want to stand, but the man in front of me gets up so I do. Cruz swings and swings and Billy covers. Cruz pushes Billy against the ropes, digs hooks to his body. Billy grabs and holds. He's looking over Cruz's shoulder, blinking, bleeding. The referee breaks them apart. Billy steps back and stops. He looks up at the lights, wipes his eye, blinks, blinks again and a bubble of blood fills the open cut then bursts. Cruz breathes deep, moves in. Billy can't see the punches coming, can't get out of the way. He throws a desperate hook that misses and Cruz counters, a straight right that snaps Billy's head and bends Billy's legs. Blood matts his hair, leaks down his cheek, drips from his chin. Cruz punches, punches. There's so much blood on the canvas it looks slick. I watch the referee call time. I watch the referee walk Billy to the doctor. I watch the doctor wipe Billy's eye to see how quickly the blood flows. He wipes the eye again and turns to the referee and shakes his head. The referee waves his arms. The fight's over. Billy Carlyle's talking to the doctor and everyone's standing, but I don't have to watch anymore. I sit.

The next fight starts. The bell rings. It rings again. It rings again.

Billy comes out of the dressing room. Some people try to shake his hand, but he keeps walking. I walk over to him. There are new stitches above his eye. There are blue bruises turning purple under his eyes. His jaw is swollen. He doesn't say anything.

We leave the Garden and walk down Seventh Avenue against traffic. The wind is cold and I put my hands in my pockets

"You got what you wanted," Billy says.

"That's not what I wanted."

"I took too many shots tonight. I have to work on not taking so many shots. My eyes can't take it."

Headlights keep coming, taxis and cars speeding uptown while the lights stay green.

"Thanks for coming," Billy says.

"You're welcome."

"I didn't know you'd be there, but it's nice to know you were."

We stop at the crosswalk to let the cars go by.

"I lost bad tonight, didn't I?"

"You lost."

"I never saw her after that one time. You have to believe me."

"I believe you."

"I got the shit beat out of me tonight and all I kept thinking about was Sam."

I look at Billy and see the opening in his eyes. His jaw tightens. He's fighting himself.

"What happened?" he says.

Billy turns from me. His wide back shakes. He moves to the building on the corner, puts his hands against the wall and throws his head forward and calls her name, pulls back his head and throws his head forward and calls her name and I'm on Billy and he throws his head into the wall and he's crying, saying he can take it, he can take it and he's crying Sam. I pull him away. I hold him. We stand in the middle of the sidewalk and move back and forth like a slow dance. I watch the headlights of the cars driving up the avenue.

I let go. The stitches are torn and blood covers his face and his blood's on me. I take a towel from his bag and press it against Billy's eye.

We take a cab to Roosevelt Hospital.

We wait in the emergency waiting room.

I watch Billy walk in.

When he comes out he's pale and the new stitches above his eye shine black under the too-bright hospital lights. His forehead is skinned and bruised.

We walk outside. Billy says he doesn't feel good. He says the body shots he took made him piss blood. He holds on to a hydrant and pukes.

We take a cab to Billy's apartment. He keeps his head between his legs. I walk him upstairs and he goes into the bathroom and pukes again. He gets into bed. He says he's so tired. I sit with him while the codeine kicks in and he breathes heavy and then his breaths come easier and he's asleep.

It's time to leave. Leave this apartment. Leave this city. Just leave. I've been thinking about California, a country's width away. Not Hollywood but somewhere warm where I can run in the mornings and go to work somewhere and the streets aren't always crowded and always fast like a punch you can't slow.

"Come on," I say like I said to the fighters tacked to the wall, *Both Members of This Club*, but quiet.

I stand.

No one's drawing.

I turn off the lights.

The dark smoothes the swelling and the stitches and the scars above his eyes and he looks almost young.

Boxing, with all its stripping down, felt like the right subject for a short novel. I want to thank the Texas Review Press for selecting Both Members of the Club *for the Clay Reynolds Novella Prize. To my agent, the late Robert Lescher, I always valued your careful attention to my writing and to me. To Craig Gardner, who came to the city when I came to the city and showed me another life—I miss you. To my great friend and colleague Jeffrey Heiman, thank you for being there to talk writing, to talk editing, and to just talk. To Frida Lee, your affection, your warmth and your smile are my best rewards. To my brother David Berlin, the boxer in the family and my closest friend, thank you for being in my corner no matter what. And to my parents, you know my thanks. Your love keeps me moving forward.*

Adam Berlin is the author of the novels *Belmondo Style* (St. Martin's Press), which won the Publishing Triangle's Ferro-Grumley award, and *Headlock* (Algonquin Books of Chapel Hill). His novel *The Number of Missing* is forthcoming from Spuyten Duyvil press. He teaches writing at John Jay College of Criminal Justice in New York City where he co-edits *J Journal: New Writing on Justice*. For more, please visit adamberlin.com.